The
Eyelid

T0018536

S. D. Chrostowska

Coach House Books, Toronto

first edition

Canada Council for the Arts
Conseil des Arts du Canada

Canada

Published with the generous assistance of the Canada Council for the Arts and the Ontario Arts Council. Coach House Books also acknowledges the support of the Government of Canada through the Canada Book Fund and the Government of Ontario through the Ontario Book Fund.

LIBRARY AND ARCHIVES CANADA CATALOGUING IN PUBLICATION
Title: The eyelid / S.D. Chrostowska.
Names: Chrostowska, S. D. (Sylwia Dominika), author.
Identifiers: Canadiana (print) 20200156608 | Canadiana (ebook) 20200156624 | ISBN 9781552454084 (softcover) | ISBN 9781770566293 (EPUB) | ISBN 9781770566385 (PDF)
Classification: LCC PS8605.H77 E94 2020 | DDC C813/.6—dc23

The Eyelid is available as an ebook: ISBN 978 1 77056 629 3 (EPUB), ISBN 978 1 77056 638 5 (PDF)

Purchase of the print version of this book entitles you to a free digital copy. To claim your ebook of this title, please email sales@chbooks.com with proof of purchase. (Coach House Books reserves the right to terminate the free digital download offer at any time.)

for Miguel Abensour, in memoriam

‘There is nothing like a dream to create the future.’

– Victor Hugo

Chapter One

Come autumn, the eyes reap colour against the lengthening shadows and the night that seals them closed, as if nature, having already given spring to love and summer to leisure, made a season especially for dreamers, its days hazy and heavy-lidded, its evenings haloed and smudged by rain, the hours' hypnotic passage sleeping all who, dazed and doubled in themselves, fall leaflike under its spell.

Men we take to be awake seem not quite so. Presentable, bright-eyed, facing the day, possibly in the habit of retiring already groomed for their appointment with tomorrow, they come upon us in our fog of somnolence and, reminded of rest, let their head sink back into the sky's great pillow, forgetting their progress. As for those with nowhere to go, or in no particular rush, they seem to have only just climbed out of bed, their clothes creased, as if yester-dusk's circadian sign had them give up their undressing, and the crack of dawn took away the reason to go on. Drowsy, practically dozing on their feet, they let their lids droop low enough to screen their dreams, with half an eye still on the noir of reality. In autumn, such absences and bifocal vision come naturally, spreading like an insuppressible yawn.

Chapter Two

I no longer remember the day we met. Unemployed for going on a year, pondering a future set agape by idleness, I had slipped by degrees into a not unpleasant state of semi-consciousness, leaving time to erode in peace what little remained of my savings. As my thoughts hewed ever closer to my surroundings, cocooned in ambient noise and newsprint, I rustled through the daily papers and, nursing a tall glass, looked out at the street teeming behind the windowpane. Childless and sans disciple, I had a corner of tedium to myself, but no life, no occupation, and no prospects to speak of, save for a standing invitation from a retired bookbinder and a psychoanalyst, an elderly couple, to visit their country estate.

I drew as much mileage as possible from this offer I could never in reality bring myself to accept. Imagining a house with its wings and empty guest rooms, a surrounding garden, and galleries stretching beneath all the way to Paris to join a mycelium of abandoned mines and catacombs, kept me going even when I myself was in no mood to budge. To languish in the capital as I did was simultaneously to while away the days until I could see myself boarding a southeasterly train sure to disembark where the air was clearer, crisper, where the grass was grizzled by frost, where the wine tasted of humus and my much-awaited hibernation could commence without further delay. My hosts, quite wrongly, presupposed in me a readiness to keep them company in their passing-house, in which time, reduced to whispers, ticked off, on a list as long as life, the varieties of pain. I had promised them nothing of the sort.

It was on one of those wet afternoons, steps fugacious on decaying matter, that my constant reverie opened wider than usual. Intoxicated by dreams of romance in a primeval forest, I had settled down on a park bench and, for all I know, had been asleep for a good half-hour, when suddenly the boards shifted beneath me, as loose or rotted ones do if another sits upon them, leading my confused mind to conclude it was the superb creature I pursued barefoot through knee-deep underbrush who, having yielded at last, came to rest, light as swan down, right beside me. I was about to discover its face.

Chapter Three

That fall, I must have seemed unusually tired. I could have slept anywhere, even slung over a rope, as they used to for three sous on Rue des Trois-Bornes. The going was no harder, although humidity and worsening pollution made it more wearisome and disagreeable, than in years past. Smog clung to my hair as to my thoughts, and I do not rule out its effects on my biography.

The day I was let go began like any other day, by the end of which nothing would be different except the headlines and the date on the calendar, were it not for that eventful loss of stability which papers over the routine of an orderly life. The post that had been mine until then suited me, and I could have sworn I had given it my all. The complaints against me cited negligence, sleeping on the clock, contagious yawning, and, by far the worst, lack of esprit de corps. What at one time required conscious effort had, I admit, become automatic, and I felt, not without reason, as if I could almost do it in my sleep. The air of inattention precipitating my dismissal was proof that I had learned to do my job too well. Having no more rules to follow with eyes closed drained me more. My bad habits, their expression capped by work, returned.

The sacking itself did not roil me enough to contest it, nor did it rouse me to put on a saving act. It was more or less expected, and perhaps desired more than less. Badly in need of rest, I received the news tranquilly, relieved rather than crestfallen. After years of blinkers and checks, a rare grade of freedom stretched out within me, my mind unsaddled by a blind emancipating hand of what I had not the strength to throw off on my own.

It was less the levitate freedom of spirit than the gravitate one to fall off the map, to let everything go, *imprimis* myself. Unsupported, no longer holding on, I took to sliding and falling, and the more I slid and fell, the heavier and wearier – objectively heavier and wearier – I became as I sank deeper into blessed sleep.

With so much latitude, my imagination, until then confined, grew bold, vivid, and complicated. In a matter of weeks, the dreamlife where I would soon pass night and day so dilated that, with the first snow, it found the last of the channels by which I still traded with reality. As white silence fell around me in flakes, taken now for poplar pollen or cotton, now for the petals of cherry blossoms, I blundered seemingly without purpose or end, as one enchanted, while underneath my lids crystallized parallel landscapes and hours lengthened to years. In this somnambulic languor, my spirits, after brief repose, became preternaturally active, as though poised on the cusp of a life-altering discovery which, I still had the sense to tell, was no more than a trick of the mind.

Chapter Four

It was by its weight, not warmth, that I first sensed the presence beside me, on a bench of wood so damp and tender as to sag toward the soil on which it stood. I raised myself and opened my eyes to a view of the pond with its two swans, a black one and a white, whose to and fro had the puissance of a pendulum to send me into a trancelike state, deepened by the water's glimmering.

Again I felt the boards move beneath my ischium, thinking myself on the scales of justice, or else on a kind of seesaw, matched against a stranger whom some unknown force, amusing itself at my expense, had placed across for counterweight to make slapstick of my efforts to touch the ground; stranded in mid-air, a sitting butt, feather-light and risible; none of it visible except, perhaps, to the two swans, which, in their ceaseless slow motion, might have registered with one eye at a time what went on ashore – so slight was my actual displacement. For a short while I struggled, fancying I could hold my own before this mute ocular quartet as it floated by. When finally I turned my head, I saw a small, unimposing man gazing out at the water.

Chapter Five

We were coated in fresh snow. Nearly awake now, I kept the silence, which seemed to envelop us, isolating me from my earlier pursuit and the drollery I had just imagined. Looking ahead at the darkening lake, I contemplated the stranger's appearance. He had the features of a child, and grey hair tousled like that of a schoolboy on recess.

My eyes, exposed to the waning daylight, adjusted to the crystals floating all around us as particles do in the liquid air of a snow globe. They wandered the length of the water's placid surface, where the swans, bowing gently toward each other, now sat motionless, the one with black feathers powdered white, the white one a dusky cast. Dubious birds of passage, these. Watching them, I was seized by a violent chill and glanced down at my overcoat to see if it was buttoned. The stranger, who stayed still the entire time and must have noticed this sudden concern with my physical condition, was more warmly dressed and, unlike me, stiff as a twig, had brushed the snow from his sleeves before it melted.

We sat together without exchanging a word, neither of us having anything to feed the swans, which drifted shoreward in our direction. To break the silence that had about it something glacial, a speechlessness that had begun to congeal into ice, I inquired, immobile, lingering in the stillness of our surroundings, for the correct time. The answer came, simple and, for one whom I took for an emissary of reality in all its permanence, sobriety, and good sense, surprisingly imprecise. And, though its tone was doleful, the stranger who shared the bench with me infused this '*Too late*' of his with a radiating warmth.

Chapter Six

He introduced himself as 'Chevauchet, diplomat.' The card he handed me, folded in half as if in confidence, gave his position as 'Ambassador of the Free Republic of Onirica,' a state, he promptly offered, virtually unknown because lacking international recognition.

In my peripheral vision, grown sharper, I thought I saw a silhouette on standby in the rushes. In the old days, in another era, a *passeur* ferried children to the rocky island over the water.

'As you well know,' said the Ambassador, interrupting my nascent reverie, 'there are many sovereign entities to whom status has historically been refused. Our republic is the last of them. It is the most foreign and the most unrecognized.'

The idea of such a scorned, outlying place resonated with me. Although I had grown up being told that I lived in the world's very centre, I always suspected its true navel to be elsewhere.

'You might not have any official and diplomatic relations with it now. But records show that most people still visit Onirica regularly and compulsively, if increasingly on the sly, keeping quiet about your travels, which, fortunately for you, require neither visas nor passports.

'You might think this would be bad for business. But for Onirica, a little outside trade with the so-called real world goes a long way. And its economy does not rely on foreign tourism. Better yet, what you leave behind and what treasures or memorabilia you bring back from your trip are yours alone. Somehow this always feels like smuggling, doesn't it? When there is really nothing to declare!

'My mission is twofold,' he resumed after a brief pause. 'To have our special statehood recognized at the highest level and as soon as possible. Then, having achieved this, and in the longer term, to work with all nations, all peoples, toward the final dissolution of the state form.'

His overture intrigued me not a little. Not only had I personally never travelled to the country he spoke of; I could not recall ever having heard of the place. And when I admitted my ignorance as to which part of the world Onirica was in, his reply was as enigmatic as the one he gave to my first question.

Chapter Seven

'*Too close,*' he again said with emphasis, more to himself this time. And, taking his hand out of his coat pocket, he cast into the lake something dark whose nature or even shape I could not make out but which, judging by the sound it had made, was a small stone or a large pebble. I made nothing of this inexplicable act, content rather in having provoked something in my bench-fellow. As starlings in flight, my thoughts swerved from him to the metaphors I knew for *disappearance,* remembering the expression *to vanish into thin air* having, in another language, its equivalent in *a stone being lost in water,* and how water closes around a sinking object like an eyelid. So Onirica lay a stone's throw away, did it? Not even across the pond? 'Then let it stay there,' I murmured spitefully to myself. 'Let it rot at the bottom of a lake.'

Casting about for something to say in return, I soon appreciated the eloquence of his wordless gesture. Though I had neither the courage nor the interest to launch into more questions, the idea of responding in kind suddenly seemed appealing. I waited for an appropriate rejoinder to come to me, wallowing as I did so in another thought, this one about the ephemeral and somewhat unreal character of conversations. The few words I had exchanged with Ambassador

Chevauchet were already fading from my memory. All that kept me from pronouncing them imaginary, besides his stubborn presence next to me and the cloud of his breath, was their warmth. They seemed significant upon being spoken but carried less weight than the stone providing punctuation and brought less clarity than the snow, which fell only to be swept away by his hand. Next to this, my confirmed inertia transformed me, in my own mind, into a fossil, so that I started when his tongue again took up the thread I had wrongly supposed broken.

'Onirica is a beautiful place, and you seem right at home in it.'

Chapter Eight

Not understanding or knowing how else to reply, I decided to play along.

'Maybe if you tell me more about Onirica I will recognize it.' I shivered as I uttered these words, feeling upon me the breath of approaching night, in whose cavernous mouth I caught sight of the uvular pendant of a waterfall.

'It is impossible to give a general description,' I heard him answer through the crashing water. 'As with any country, everything depends on your location and place in it. Take Greater America. What it looks like to you has little in common with what it is to a Chinese factory-villager, or a prisoner in Oaxaca, or a Parisian schoolchild, or a New York banker, or an imam in Africa, or an aborigine in Arnhem Land. Yet you all occupy one and the same world-state. Onirica, too, is heterogeneous, contingent on where one is coming from.

'That said, in Onirica, social inequalities and the pressures of individual circumstances back home are mostly non-existent. Once inside, your mindset is not decisive for what happens to you. Of course, in one crucial sense, Onirica depends on your mental state: you cannot recognize it awake!

'But perhaps we can do something about that…' he said, turning to face me. 'What do you think of to fall asleep? Do you shuffle cards, count sheep…?'

'Neither,' I answered without conviction. 'I always picture two swans, a black and a white one, just like those in front of us, gliding toward each other and then, very slowly, entwining together their long necks. I never reach the point when they strangle themselves, or each other. I seem to drop off just in time to avoid seeing it. Imagining this scene has never once failed to anaesthetize me.' The idea, invented on the spot, pleased me, and I made a mental note to give it a try.

'What about your other habits?' he persevered. 'Do you sleep well, on the whole?'

In fact, I was embarrassed about my lassitude of late. I slept not only well but in excess. He must have noted my unease at the question.

'I can, of course, guess some things outright. For instance, you seem a bit tired. But you would be remarkably fresh for someone who did not get enough sleep. Do I gather from this that you regularly have a good night's rest and that last night was an exception? Not at all. It seems to me, rather, that you habitually sleep more than you need, over and above what is strictly necessary, and even that, for some time now, you may have been caught in a spiral of sleep. Am I wrong?'

I nodded, unable to stifle the yawn breaking across my face.

'In your case, then,' he went on, 'Onirica is a vast land of abundance, wonder, and adventure. A country of open borders, across which you travel freely and frequently. A place where, in every port, a table and a bed await you. Whose inhabitants fascinate you. Where everyone, including you, enjoys unheard-of freedom of expression. Where boredom is unknown. Where your wishes, even the most inadmissible, come true.'

I smiled at his fable and saw floating in the distance, like an Italian landscape, what he had just sketched in a few deft strokes. All at once, I felt the bench sink slightly on my end – a spur to get up as well. As I rose to my feet, I discovered I was no longer in a park overlooking a pond but facing the door of a house. I found the bell and rang it instinctively.

'Welcome to Onirica,' Chevauchet greeted me as he appeared on the other side of the threshold. 'It is a pleasure to host someone of your oneiric talents. We can continue our conversation here.' He motioned for me to come in.

But for the floor creaking, the house was quiet. I sat down at the table he had set for us and helped myself to the lavish spread – and to the wine, that truthful soporific. Chevauchet's voice grew muffled, like a radio played downstairs or underwater, or damped with felt. The napkin with which I still managed to wipe my lips was so fine it must have been made of eyelashes. Overcome by a wave of fatigue, forgetting my manners, I rested my head on it. Out of the corner of my eye, I saw a grey dog wander in from an adjacent room and curl up beside the fireplace, and, before I knew it, I was sound asleep.

I awoke in a strange bed to find Chevauchet sitting at the foot of it. He appeared to be waiting for me, intent on speaking.

'Do you mind if I lie here and listen to you?' I asked, hoping to continue drifting in and out of consciousness.

'Be my guest,' he replied, evidently pleased with my request.

'Sleep, you must know,' he began, 'has never been more maligned than in our time. It matters little that its physiological necessity and benefits for health remain scientifically undisputed. Who nowadays applauds the committed sleeper? What employer rewards employees for sleep? Talk about heaven on earth!

'Very few see any merit in sleeping, and those who still do don't dare admit it. Even health, physical and mental well-being, has its limits. Sleep *may be useful in some cases,* that is the most anyone is openly willing to give it – such caution has become characteristic of the subject. Anything in excess of the old social norm, the prescribed six hours, is deemed prodigal.

'Why is sleep equated with sloth, with good-for-nothingness? The answer is obvious. For the moment, the economy has not found a way to capture it. Sleep is excessive when it exceeds the bounds of the system, as it invariably does when we dream.

'The system has not yet managed to integrate sleeping subjects for active exploitation, as producers and consumers of goods. It has combatted laziness by filling it with artificial paradises. But it does not know what to do with the odd Saint-Pol-Roux, who declares that his work consists in sleeping. A fool, clearly!

'Almost everyone now sees virtue in insomnia, a word once associated with pathology, with disorder. It is more desirable than all the drugs taken together to make one forget the troubles of this world. Wilful insomniacs may be users, hooked on uppers, but they are more useful than sleepers. Everyone places a premium on awareness, scared of missing something vital to survival. They tell themselves that missing something can be the difference between life and death. There is a reason sleep is a euphemism for death. Sleeping is no longer considered a privilege, a luxury, since hardly anyone these days wants to or can afford it. And as bad as the situation is, it is early days yet. Things will only get worse. Much worse.

'Those in power know that sleep is a time of freedom. Dreams awaken us to the possibility of another world, which can be enough to give us hope for it, if not always a vision of real liberty. Sometimes all we have left is hope. It is then all the more precious. And sometimes we have a wish but no hope of its coming true. Thanks to dreams, the strange glimpses they offer, we have at least a notion of freedom.

'Was there a time when we didn't dream of better places? Or of a world far from suffering and death? We are utopian animals. The dream of death's overcoming, of awakening beyond eternal, dreamless sleep, we dream with open eyes. In sleep, we realize it. We close our real eyes to open them again in a dream, where death, which only happens in reality, cannot reach us, where we are unavailable to it.'

Absorbing his words, I stretched and rubbed my eyes, then looked out the window. It was dawning, and on a pond visible through the glass I discerned a pair of black swans. Farther out, the sails of several windmills turned listlessly, surrounded by cattle, couchant and levant, upon a hill. I could not tell if we were still in the city, at the embassy, or in a house in the countryside. Chevauchet's voice emerged from within the room, though he himself did not materialize:

'In Onirica, you see, we are asleep and awake at the same time. But we need sleep just as we need waking life. They are inseparable. It is wrong to exploit sleep: to sleep in the service of life, in order to live. It upsets a natural balance.

'As soon as you turn something into a means, its value in itself is put into question. Dreaming for its own sake – without some ulterior motive, some enhancement of life – holds no more worth. You are approaching a state of absolute sleeplessness, without even realizing it, because what you value above everything else is being conscious. The rest – sleeping, dreaming, idleness – seems primitive by comparison, the preserve of unreason, of myth. The way things are going, you will get rid of it all soon enough.'

Chapter Nine

If this had been the nineteenth century, the golden age of insurrection, he would have been a professional revolutionary, an agitator of dreams. But in this world where great, sweeping changes could be wrought only by compromise and multilateral co-operation, a world in which dreams were like all other things – for sale, existing only to be fulfilled, and otherwise without the right to exist – he could make himself useful only in diplomacy.

Chevauchet, 'ambassador' of dreams that could be neither bought nor possessed, strictly immaterial, and given away in this form to kindred spirits; dreams that could still be dreamt rather than had, because reality would not have them – aspirations that exceeded it, wishes that ran contrary to it that it would never grant; dreams that not only escaped the frenzied production of simulacra but threatened to lay waste, one idol at a time, to the great marketplace of fantasies. He wanted to bring this illicit, shadow economy into the light by legalizing its source – a 'republic,' a place real enough, even if its sole good was involuntary make-believe.

'Real enough' were his words, not mine. Onirica was real enough for making dreams. These needed reality as much as reality needed them.

'It is thanks to people like you' – he pointed to me, his slight figure drawn out of the shadows by the pale morning sun – 'that dream and reality can still communicate.

'Daydreams are my outpost in reality, my embassy. Autumn is when I am busiest. But I keep busy all year round, and lately around the clock. I am lucky to have found you. You say little and you listen. You may be the most dream-prone person I have come across. A natural ally. What you dream of is less important than *that* you dream and keep dreaming. And here in Onirica, the dream state to which you have followed me, we can talk shop. I am proposing a collaboration.'

I opened my mouth, but he resumed before I could agree or protest.

'My diplomacy is public, directed not at leaders and senior government officials but at ordinary private citizens, lotus-eaters like yourself. I often meet them on work breaks or solitary strolls in parks, where city people go to dream.

'In parks, fantasy beckons. They have a special charm. By day, greenery, the open air, the sunshine evoke rest. At dusk, the colours come alive, more vibrant than in the movies. After dark, the beds of grass cushion sleeplessness, my *bête noire*, and the moon casts its shadow plays ...'

Listening to him energized me.

'Yes!' I ejaculated. 'I would always rather paint the night white with solitary wanderings than red with trouble!'

'I am glad to hear it,' he replied, amusedly. 'But keep in mind there are different shades of red. And different ways of painting it.'

Chapter Ten

In the following adventures – as he liked to call them – Chevauchet made himself my Virgil, a genial cicerone through the circles of Hell and along the terraces of Purgatory, raising my hopes of Paradise. The geography of Onirica in no wise resembled the place I remembered reading about in Greek class, at an age when something encountered in a book could still leave an indelible impression.

It was in a story by Lucian of Samosata, where he recounts his visit to the Isle of Dreams, *hē tōn oneirōn nēsos* – the same that Homer, in *The Odyssey,* calls the land of *dēmos oneirōn,* or dream-people. When first sighted, the island appears 'dim and uncertain to the eye.' In this it is much like its inhabitants. Indeed, the closer one came to it, muses Lucian, the more it 'receded and retired and retreated to a greater distance.' How such an infinite approach eventually culminates in landfall he does not explain. It just happens, as impossible things often do in dreams.

Lucian and his companions disembark at dusk in a harbour named Sleep. To reach the city, they must pass through a wood, which surrounds it on all sides. The trees in this forest are enormous poppies and lofty mandrakes, narcotic plants both, and the only birds in it are bats (the call of an owl or the song of a nightingale being too disruptive). Their path takes them past the river Sleepwalker and two springs, Twelve-Hours and Soundly. When they finally enter the city, whose walls are rainbow-coloured, it is through a gate made of ivory, which signifies dreams that deceive, finding no fulfillment in reality. This is but one of four gates, the others being of horn, for dreams that come to pass in reality and inspire action; of iron, and of earthenware, these last meant especially for dreams that are 'frightful and murderous and revolting.'

Once inside the city, Lucian's party admires the temple of Night and the palace of Sleep, the ruler of all dreams, whose two satraps are Nightmare, the son of Vacuity, and Rich, the son of Fancy. A further two temples, dedicated to Trick and to Truth, house their 'holy of holies and their oracle.' Finally, in a memorable passage, our Syrian narrator and guest describes the isle's inhabitants, in all their singularity and diversity:

> *Some were tall, handsome, and pleasant to look at, others short and malformed; some seemed rich, while others humble and poor. There were also among them winged and monstrous ones, and others dressed up as kings and gods and the like, as if going to a procession. We actually recognized many, having seen them long ago back where we came from. These came up to us and greeted us like old acquaintances, took us with them, put us to sleep quite splendidly, and entertained us hospitably in their homes. They treated us like lords in every way and even promised to make us kings and satraps. A few of them took us*

home, gave us a glimpse of our families, and brought us back the same day.

Onirica had nothing of the solidity, definition, or autonomy of the Isle of Dreams – this despite the fact that, unlike Lucian and his gang, I was shown around by its envoy, an insider set on giving me a guided tour. Two millennia lay between but did not separate our stories. I knew no more than they did what to expect.

Chapter Eleven

The day came and went, its hours unaccounted for, and before long, evening was upon us again. Darkness, rather than descending in its usual curtainfall fashion, seeped in from below like India ink, absorbed by the landscape. It was time to go, for the park was about to close, and it would be a nuisance if municipal keys were to lock us in.

'Is anyone expecting you?' Chevauchet asked, more out of politeness, seeing I was in no obvious hurry to part ways. At my negative reply, he visibly perked up.

'Come then,' he said, getting up from our bench. 'I have something less run-of-the-mill to offer than a café, and at no cost. Does seeing inside other people's dreams appeal to you?'

I voiced my reservations: was it not too intrusive, a breach of privacy, even if it were nowhere explicitly prohibited as trespassing? He dispelled my worries with a critique of privacy as a bourgeois invention.

'Of course, I cannot guarantee tonight will be a great show. But we won't know what that is unless we see what's playing. By the way, no oneiroscopes required!'

We walked the perimeter of the lake, which shone in the moonlight like a Claude glass. As we passed the grotto with its cascade on our way to the exit, it suddenly felt as if we had crossed an invisible threshold. And right then, I saw, hovering like a hologram and spotlit as on a stage a few paces ahead of me, a young man kneeling beside the bed of a girl, who was sleeping.

'A dream of love,' whispered Chevauchet.

The scene and the man's comportment did indeed suggest ardent emotion, a love-melancholy fired by loss. The pallor of his beloved hinted she was on her deathbed. He held her hand, frowned, then wept. Only love can come this close to death without flinching. I saw his desire for union with her throwing a bridge over the chasm now dividing them to a life together beyond the grave.

He was offering the girl a rose. Its thorns were making him bleed. He tried handling it through a sheet, but this was too fine not to be pierced as well. Was his love a rose that hurt him unawares? One he had not learned to handle without pain? Was the blushing and prickly flower supposed to bring her back to life, return her to herself? Or was it a farewell? He seemed to me less a masochist than a knight, with his flowering chivalry.

'They don't make them that way anymore,' said Chevauchet, as if reading my mind. The lover's love was stronger than his lust, his devotion stronger than his passion. The worm was no match for him. These thoughts came to me telepathically, vicariously.

I knew also, though I could not say how, that this was the selfsame rose he had refused to purchase from an insistent peddler, who kept lowering the price until, more in mockery than frustration, he threw it away. The young man felt insulted, put to shame by the beggar. And she, what did she see? In that red rose she must have seen herself. And the rose he was presenting to her now, when it was too late, was less a declaration of his feelings than a token of his regret, a confession of guilt. He did not love her enough. The drops of blood from his fingers stained the bedclothes, while his tears left no trace. Did he blame himself for losing her?

And by a rose, as if by free association, we passed into a dream-vision of socialism. Its older floral symbol, still wedded to the International Workers' Day, was the carnation. But, as I found out from Chevauchet, the rose and the love of freedom and equality had a much longer and richer history together. The flower meant secrecy, resistance, and, speaking with its thorns, opposition to unjust authority. I shall make you suffer if you lay your hands on me, it seemed to say.

The rose we saw said nothing, and instead of thorns was possessed of two red fists, which it brought down furiously upon a tortoise shell, great and detailed as a world in miniature. The tortoise had managed to duck and hide its head; it was safe from the blows. And as the rose kept pummelling away, to no apparent avail, its fists became bloody like hunks of meat on spits.

I could no longer bear the sight of blood. Why were night-dreams so violent, even when they were about love?

Chapter Twelve

Our next stop was along the same trajectory, but in territory that was new to me.

'Onirica's Avenue des Cauchemars,' announced Chevauchet. As its name implied, a favourite setting for nightmares.

We trod the littered pavement, rats scurrying to every side from overturned dumpsters and groans issuing from the tenements – timeless urban scenery, in which the props change little.

'Dreams of dread,' he resumed, taking up a by-now-familiar thread, 'are like a dream within a dream within a dream. The trace of pre-existing fear intensifies to the point of conjuring for itself a cause, which incites still greater fright, surpassing that cause, and so on.'

One of its victims, explained Chevauchet as we climbed several steep flights of back stairs, lived with his family in the attic of this building (his parents being entertainers). He had observed the little boy earlier that afternoon, inconsolable, having just suffered one of those infantile misfortunes for which poverty is most to blame: his jam sandwich had fallen face down on the kitchen terracotta – the ubiquitous hexagonal tiles his father christened 'the Frances of Roaches.'

Chevauchet expected this episode to colour the boy's dreams that night.

We approached. By now the boy was breathing like one fast asleep. And in his dream he found himself just outside his apartment. He was there because his father was rehearsing his flea circus, while his mother sang. The zigzag of the corridor, which he was still too little to explore alone right to the end, gave him the creeps. He stood on the landing and stared fixedly into the dark hallway when his fear got the better of him.

Rolling languidly through the shadows, past the six or seven *chambres de bonne* where his neighbours lived, past the recessed common sink and the gas and water conduits trained on an espalier like ivy, through the dense cigarette smoke snaking toward him between bannister posts, quite close now, was the head of the giant Goliath, its course marked by a trail of slime and blood. Seeing it, the boy became rooted to the spot, petrified by the gruesome apparition. Then, snapping out of it, he screamed and fell back, and as he began falling down the stairwell, he awoke with a gasp. We stood by, waiting until he was asleep again. He sensed nothing of our presence.

The next dream cycle, still under the sign of nightmares, was a variation on this theme. The boy dreamt of sleeping in a large hall, the foyer of a mansion, or maybe a skyscraper. In his dream, he had just grasped his dire situation: he was in the dark all by himself. He pulled the blanket over his ears. Suddenly, he felt, or imagined feeling, a strange hand cross the bed toward him like a great spider. Not knowing where to turn, he cowered and began howling – *Awwoooooo!*

awwoooooo! awwoooooo! Awwooooo! – sounds a cartoon wolf makes, so pitiful were they.

It did not help that the hand now belonged to a deaf-blind gentleman who had lost his cane, and all his bearings in effect, and so deserved pity himself. The bed was his lifeline, human contact his only hope. And it seemed obvious somehow that when his tremulous fingers finally touched the boy, they would become the boy's, yet experienced – impossibly – as those of a stranger.

Awwooooo! Awwoooo! the little wolf went on hysterically, lacking the power of discernment, unable to hear anything but his own distress. Feeling sorry for him, covering my ears – I really could stand no more of the child's lament, and imagined his terror when the tenacious hand took hold of him – I urged us on, desperate by that point for a change of scene.

At this, Chevauchet made a gesture as if pushing aside a veil, and we passed quickly through a sort of hall of dreams that reminded me a lot of dioramas, or what they used to call *entre-sorts,* except that they were live. We left one and, still impressed by its forms and colours, directly stepped into another, which revealed itself like a slide projection, a fresh backdrop, or an old layer of wallpaper. The scenes we left behind continued playing, as it were, sans audience, in the privacy of their dreamers, while the scenes we set foot in unfolded around us like the pages of a pop-up book. But since we did not stop for quite a while, we were moving through them as they kept moving, so that our way of seeing was unlike taking in a film or a conventional piece of theatre.

Seeing me take fright, Chevauchet turned to me and said, 'You are perhaps beginning to understand why I want to unite nightmares, which are awful, and daydreams, which are generally pleasant.' And he told me of nightmares that 'run in families' and that sheer repetition renders unshakable.

To take the nearest example, the elder brother of the wolf boy we had caught falling had long been harassed by the same bad dream. He was in a wood-panelled room with thick Persian carpeting when he would hear a noise coming from beneath the floor. Curious, he would lift the rugs, heavy and dust-packed, and, no nearer the source of the mysterious scratching, pry loose the floorboards, which splintered. This still not unravelling the mystery, he would dig even deeper, under the room, clearing away the dirt with his hands. At which point he would remember the curse and, as panic tunnelled his vision, realize that he too must now be struck down by the Egyptian pharaoh, whose secret tomb he had disturbed – to be buried in it.

The recurring nightmare of the boys' mother, which Chevauchet narrated for me, was altogether more unsettling for hewing closer to actual history – its darkest chapter, to boot.

It started off innocuously. She dreamt of herself as a pubescent girl in a wing chair vis-à-vis an old woman. The matron was a member of the Wagner clan – one of Richard's grandchildren – by then too innocent and senile to play a Valkyrie. Her heart and the only part of her memory still intact belonged to the Third Reich, when she was young and attractive. She pronounced *Reich* like a talisman, savouring it, making her young listener cringe.

At one point, the girl, who was Jewish, would be shown an antique pocket watch. It was expensive, a personal gift from the Führer! The girl could not understand all that the old woman was telling her in beaming, toothless German. But she nevertheless grasped enough to know that both Hitler and his Minister of Propaganda used to pay calls to this very room in courtship. Each had taken tea in the very armchair that now held her hostage. She looked closer at the watch and out jumped the dedication: *The bigger the lie, the better it works. Yours, Adi.* The dream always ended there, in shock.

In the same vein, the mother dreamt of having been condemned to death by the Gestapo. The SS officer ordered to execute her liked to do it in his billet. To avoid some kind of inspection (there was a knock on the door), he would shove her into a shallow chest of drawers, where she would lie, folded flat like a sweater, until the coast was clear. When it was okay to do so, he would let her out. Afraid he would now 'do the deed,' she would appeal to his humanity, imploring him not to kill her: 'I can stay put in this drawer for hours' – and she would fold herself neatly again – 'Like so!' 'The war will be over any day now!' (it was the winter of 1944), she reasoned with the man from the SS. She would open the other drawers, feeling at home. The deepest one, on the bottom, contained her woollens. It was infested with moths. So none could escape, she proceeded to spray everything with the insecticide Kapo®. This complicity in the killing made her feel safe. But the gaping holes in her best sweater knew different ...

Chapter Thirteen

Just as Chevauchet was wrapping up his account of the dream, we dismounted from our pegasus, deposited as if on request at a chalet or country inn. It was a Golden Lion, Lion d'Or, a rare sight these days. A bell somewhere struck midnight.

We checked in at reception and, in search of a warm meal, made our way over to the restaurant. We sat down and ordered. Busy conversing with the other guests at our table, I did not at first see the dwarf who had planted himself at my elbow. He hung on patiently until, following the glances of Chevauchet, who sat across from me, I took notice of him. At this, he placed in my lap an amputated finger. It did not appear to have been severed per se, but detached whole like putty. The messenger grinned idiotically, then turned around and left.

I asked Chevauchet what it meant, to which he replied sheepishly that it was up to me: 'After all, it is your dream.' Queasy, I called a waiter and sent the finger back like a dish that disagreed with me. Within minutes, the little man was at my side again and dropped the finger, Dalíesque and éclair-like, back in my lap. This farce repeating several more times without explanation, I decided to take matters into my own hands, chased him out of doors, and returned to finish my dinner. Only then did it dawn on me that, like the singer of 'Les Feuilles mortes' in *Gates of the Night,* I may have belittled a warning from fate, leaving it no choice but to teach me a lesson.

Before we retired to bed, I asked Chevauchet to explain to me our mode of travel and what spying on the dreams of strangers was meant to serve. It was a question he had apparently anticipated; he laid out his thinking reasonably and succinctly.

Dream-hopping, as he called what we did, would, if generalized, build community, and not just among individual dreamers but also among their figments – those they themselves dreamt into existence and would want to associate with. These phantoms would be 'dependents,' and a shared responsibility.

Diplomacy, of the kind Chevauchet had undertaken, could succeed only by such activity. Where real life demanded passports, here only a passe-partout would do. All should enjoy right of passage through the dreams and daydreams of others, on condition that they abstained from meddling in them. Such passage already occurred between one's own dreams and daydreams. They were 'our own' in name only, being in no way our property. We could not even be certain of being their makers. And since dreams neither really belonged nor were original to us, a dream-community ought to be possible.

As the restaurant slowly emptied for the night, our attention was drawn to the television playing in the background. Below the image of a news anchor, a message scrolled across the screen: *Unsafe tunnel, extreme temperatures, and vermin make recovery of bodies and search for evidence difficult.* Then the words *UP NEXT: Chrysanthemums, or the Day of the Bombs*, which I took to be the title of a late-night feature.

The eye of the camera panned across a black-and-white landscape: a misty orchard, its trees frosted over, bare and gnarled. From a distance they made a stereogram pattern. In fact, the story, of which this was the opening sequence, had the faint contour of a bas-relief figure hidden in a repeating-panel picture, each of its individual segments, on the contrary, sharp as in a camera obscura.

Next, I saw a paysage covered in chrysanthemums the size of cabbage heads. The entire horticultural zone seemed enclosed in a kind of bubble. The flowers were vividly hued and, similar to crepe paper, rough to the touch. They were being cultivated like so many shrines. Above them extended an astonishing Oz-like skyscape, the clouds wildly polychromatic and transmuted in ever-changing variations, as in a kaleidoscope. They had a colouring-book appearance. Nearer to the ground, a warm breeze rustled the treetops, shaking out the dust. There was no one about; only later did I spot people kneeling at chrysanthemum patches, attending to them like sextons or altar boys, or walking, heads bent, around a cabbage field, of the ornamental variety (the cold, if not severe, enhanced its colour). Every now and then, a noiseless, solitary cyclist would cut across a vista of strapping conifers. Sunshine as on a late-spring or early-autumn day illuminated the forest in shafts. Along the rim of it ran a plain country road, down which we headed.

Little by little, a gigantic rubber sphere came into view on the horizon. A glossy, purple-brown ball the size of a strawberry moon, it came bouncing over hills. According to announcements made over the airwaves, it was the fallout from the bombings of several American cities. Buffalo was the first hit. An intertitle informed: *The Tragedy at Buffalo.*

The newscasts reached me as through invisible loudspeakers concealed in the clouds. Their volume was the same everywhere, the announcer's voice booming overhead. But drowning it out near the ground was the hum of a nuclear plant, or of a distant stampede of buffalo. I saw no installation or transmission towers anywhere, yet the atmosphere was maximally charged.

The road led to a block of flats, winding long like a train, and to arrive at the very last unit took some time. The air inside was pure and sterile. The furnishings were minimal: a chair, a bed, and a bicycle, as if to suggest a getaway.

On the white wall, next to a poster for the Pan-American Exposition of 1901, I made out the following nostalgic verse, presumably composed before the attack by the room's last tenant:

A horror ran up my leg and lodged itself in my brain.
Remember when we had no need of bullhorns?
It was enough to speak.
Those days have fallen silent.
This is not a prophecy.

The lines gave way to an 'Indian-head' test pattern.

Chapter Fourteen

We were now above the great park, and the ink in the sky was fading. I was puzzled by the way time seemed to compress and expand in Chevauchet's company.

'It must be about seven o'clock,' I hazarded.

'So it is,' he replied, visibly excited. 'The witching hour of dreams of power!'

Down below, we saw an arena in which two naked men were locked in hand-to-hand combat. We descended and blended into the crowd observing the fight. The people assembled were clearly plebians, whereas the fighters appeared to belong to the noble caste. Their skin was painted gold; beneath the paint it was black. From one of the onlookers we learned that, in these parts, when the king died (as happened recently), the chiefs met to choose a new leader. Confounding cruelty with bravery, they made their head the fiercest one among them. During the past nine days, said the commoner, their exploits took the form of duels with POWs or criminals, then with one another. He who showed himself the most valiant or terrible, capable of the greatest violence, would henceforth be feared as the greatest in the nation and be named king. He would be given a triumphant welcome in his future palace, where new trials and excesses awaited him, lasting another nine days. Although it was not given to the masses to witness it, intemperance and debauchery would there be taken to such an extreme that the new ruler almost invariably succumbed, and the ceremonial would start over. It was rare for the festival not to cost the lives of many men, concluded our dream-interlocutor on a note of grand pathos.

This was 'The Spectacle to End All Spectacles.' For centuries now, the ritual had kept the number of tyrants to a bare minimum.

We moved away and spied the dream's dreamer pressing through the crowd to get closer to the contestants, one of whom had just lost an ear and roared like a wild beast. Then our man did something bizarre: he entered the arena and lay himself down flat on the ground like a log, and waited in this position to be trampled to death.

'Seems to me more like a dream of impotence!' I remarked to Chevauchet.

'A desire too long repressed can, in a dream, turn into its opposite; disappointed dreams give birth to their contraries. The dialectic of wishing is delicate and unpredictable.' The pensive tone of his response implied I had chanced upon something fundamental, a vulnerability in the mechanism that was also, however, its strength.

With this ended the first of my many visits to Onirica.

Chapter Fifteen

Diplomacy was the righteous upright cousin of double agency. It required being simultaneously in two states. With one foot in dreamy Onirica, the other in waking Fantasy, folded in two like a folio, Chevauchet straddled both. Or rather, he worked in their overlap.

And just as each leaf had its other half somewhere pages apart, so each night-dream had, if I understood him right, its counterpart, its 'distant double,' in reverie. But what were dreams? He was averse to such general definitions. The most he would venture was that they were singular and that they constituted a realm of individual freedom even when all other freedoms had been stripped and collective freedom taken away. Yet this liberty was not what we were used to calling 'autonomy.' It was, he insisted, 'isonomic' – ordering blanket equality and allowing us to imagine, beyond, or beneath, individuals, an undifferentiated 'collective unconscious.' Such unconscious was neither real nor unreal, and neither true nor false.

The freedom in dreams was likewise not a negative, escapist one. Night and day, the dreamer remained bound to reality. Night-dreams were in thrall to the past. At the same time, they were unfettered from official history, the artificial continuity of the past. Binding dreamers were the details of the lives they had lived, things insignificant or unnoticeable, subconscious or forgotten. It was inventory from this past, and not their personal 'stories,' that lay its dead hand upon them and gave them nightmares. This past, and not official history, held them in its grip, and did not keep them awake at night but, on the contrary, tenaciously asleep.

It was a strange kind of freedom, but it was freedom nonetheless. And what held true for nocturnal dreams in this respect was even truer of reveries: they were mental islands of liberty, even for the isolated. Chevauchet liked to refer to the sixteenth-century philosopher Étienne de La Boétie on matters of freedom, and did so in this case. Should a tyrant take the liberty of action away from us, so we could no longer communicate our aspirations or even think clearly, we would still be free in our daydreams. Only, we would be isolated in them. Our reveries would, in effect, make our enslavement and tyranny unbearable, reinforcing the prison we once took for a citadel. This might push us to break out in search of company. On the other hand, when extreme isolation was sought voluntarily, and our mind revolved around ideals, the freedom of such reverie was squandered, put in the service of an imaginary heaven for one.

Reveries were linked to aspiration, to projects and hopes. They were optative, future-directed, but whether they had a future depended entirely on whether their dreamer was ready to chase them, and on how far they were prepared to go.

For Chevauchet, the future 'belonged' to daydreams.

They were the core of his *unified theory of utopia* (as naive and idealistic as this sounded). Dreaming was no more *intrinsically totalitarian* than awakening – under the name of 'class consciousness' – was *inherently revolutionary*, leading to emancipation. Speculative utopian blueprints and abstractions left him cold. Utopia was quite simply the plurality of dissonant dreams and poetic traditions, chief among them being Romanticism and Surrealism. These utopian currents awoke latent myths containing values of the unjustly silenced, the vanquished – values that any oppressed could claim and incarnate, bringing to life in such manner past struggles and lost causes, redeeming them. This kept the sphere of action open for universalization. But values could also be co-opted, turned against themselves, dialectically reappropriated. They were in constant danger of ending up as grist or caught in the 'birdlime' of ideology.

'Only in dreams can we still act, can there still be any real change.' By this he meant that we could change the world for the better only through, or by way of, wishful thinking that 'awakened' our potential for unrest. Real wakefulness, however, was the enemy. And the aim was not revolution as we know it. Our resistance to the system could only take shape where one overthrew the symbolic order of reality: in a united dreamworld. Only there could its 'vanishing lines' be seen. 'Another world exists: inside this one,' he would repeat, quoting Paul Éluard. 'Dream what you would like to become reality,' he would add himself, with last-words finality.

Chapter Sixteen

At first, I did not see how diplomacy could go hand in hand with fomenting revolution. Granted, the one Chevauchet prepared was non-violent and would take place entirely within dream states. In the crudest terms, so I could comprehend it, the mission was to unite night- with daydreams, the tension between them being at a breaking point. Its main obstacle was always the fear that reveries would slip control if one ceded too much ground to their nocturnal others. Night-dreams were widely held to be exotic country, a lawless dimension of the past that, once visited, served no purpose, but only revived or reinforced undesirable memories. The Onirican 'republic' was pure anarchy. It mattered little that criminal wishes could as readily bloom in the so-called free and conscious mind, their roots planted firmly in the soil of reverie. By condemning night-dreams as illogical and immoral, dreamers closed their eyes to the same in their woolgathering.

What was immoral was servitude, which did not exist in dreams. Wilful enslavement was the norm everywhere the 'emperor' was invisible.

'Servitude is no less servile for being voluntary,' Chevauchet would say. 'Willing it only makes the bondage more profound. You accept state coercion in exchange for the ability to act on your selfish urges, available as a shrinking set of options. Captive minds, sworn to inaction, generally give up thinking of vengeance, treason, revolt, and crime. You congratulate yourselves on your impeccable morality, even if purchased at so high a price. Your easy conscience lets you sleep at night. But dreams are where you give yourselves over to wickedness with impunity and where you stow the skeletons. Where you allow yourself to be ravished by incubi and succubi. Dreams do your dirty work. They are the theatre for your private catharsis. So you disown them.

'Meanwhile, little by little, you give in to the lure of insomnia to make you still more upstanding, still more efficient and productive, to the detriment of creativity. You sacrifice sleep and, with it, your dreams. And what if you could not sleep *at all*? What if that guilty pleasure was denied you, knowing that, in your willed servitude, you would not resist? Would your conscience be as clear then? Would you not, then, rise up to defend your right to sleep – which is as much as saying "your right to dream"? You would realize that dreaming was not only your private underworld, but your last scrap of freedom as well. By then, of course, it would be too late. Because you would have already traded in sleep for money. You are constantly aided and nudged to cut down on it. All the propaganda is bound to take and make insomnia desirable. You seem to forget that losing sleep will, over time, cost you not just your dreams but also your daydreams, and ultimately even thinking creatively, what is called "thinking for yourself." It is just a question of when.

'Sleep is a foundation, period. It is under siege. We need to protect it.'

Chapter Seventeen

Chevauchet's monologues were never rants. Despite his mounting foreboding, he carried himself with utmost composure. If he had official status then, he would already have been expelled, as all ties of Greater America with the land of sleep were being definitively severed. He knew about these disquieting developments, state secrets at that point, long before the public did. If anyone could access top-level fantasies and power trips, it was he.

As with any drastic measures, there was bureaucratic inertia and reaction in some sectors of the government. It would be months before everyone there was on the same page; and months before stepped-up economic policies, leaked to the press, triggered the creation of new supervisory agencies to instate censorship; months, as well, before they were implemented and functionalized; and months again before popular initiatives of mass distraction appeared in their true light, if only to the few conscious enough to infer their effects on civil society.

'Empire of the Mind' was the latest experiment in the field of Comprehensive Illusion (CI), aiming to institutionalize daydreaming. The program already interfaced with reality, allowing subscribers – which would soon mean every registered household – to realize their dreams by constructing virtual environments deceptively close to the actual. (The first to be granted free basic access were displaced peoples, eco-refugees, to divert their attention from life in the camps.) In this pluralistic daydream, everything was possible. Individual fantasies became mutually reconcilable. The new dispensation did away with the unity of time and space, and gave citizens leave to stretch reality as far as it would go.

The free-for-all engendered by this ostensible loosening of laws had no bearing on the real world, where social bonds were disintegrating. The fantasies entrusted to CI were contained by it, centrally monitored, analyzed, and disarmed. With a mere tweak of the algorithm, all potential threats to the new order were nipped in the bud.

Reality, meanwhile, was run ultra-rationally, with galloping and uncompromising efficiency. In it, all were about to become slaves to their own sanitized fancies. In the most recent upgrade to security, everything was encrypted, tamper- and foolproof. Whatever facilitated policing was sold as just one more step to ensure privacy. But the fact of the matter was that, as part of an effort to thwart terrorism and other political activities in CI, individual daydreams, though they remained interactive, became immune to peer influence and criticism. This would soon apply across the board – to all reveries – since everyone who hadn't yet done so wanted to transition to CI's flashier, more stimulating and rewarding, less fatiguing environment. *Natural reveries* were work – work that, being merely 'creative,' got in the way of true, profitable productivity. Daydreaming in cyberspace was assisted and augmented; it was easier. (The more data CI gathered on its users, the faster it relieved them of inputting new material.) As a result, it took up much less time. The mediated experiences it enabled were richer and exponentially more concentrated. There needed no better incentive. Addiction to CI could not but bring forth a more docile and impotent public.

In such a climate, Chevauchet's subliminal labours fell short of their aim. For how could those whose dreams in a sense came true, and whose de facto masters came up with imaginative ways to keep them happy, designing a playground of desire that at the same time corralled it – how could they possibly be convinced that this wish-granting virtual reality was to be resisted rather than embraced and celebrated? And, in a sense, they might be right not to be. Did not *all* daydreams, and not just these 'artificial' ones, substitute for action? Had not all imagination always colluded with existing conditions, altering reality as little as possible, accommodating and compensating for its flaws? Was not a stable reality indispensable to sanity? And finally, was not reality itself a great construction, which might founder as soon as credibility was withdrawn from it by those who were its citizens? Would not the fantasy-world prevail someday, reversing the hierarchy – when partakers of reality died out, and their children, averse to its hard consequences, deemed it too dangerous, unpredictable, and irreversible by comparison? If all migrated to CI, what would be left of the powers that be? Over whom would they rule? Their sole legitimacy would derive from running CI. They would not dare shut it down and risk real rebellion. In the end, being only human, they too would jump ship, abandoning the nave of reality, and, crossing over, incapable of deferring any further the satisfaction offered by CI, would live out their fantasies of power unchecked as never before. With this, the state as such would wither away, die a natural death, and the universal statelessness Chevauchet was after would be a *fait accompli*. The great unmooring from reality would be justified once reality itself was no longer anchored securely but set adrift.

Chevauchet's reaction to my reverie (for I was not playing devil's advocate) was 'Keep dreaming!' and it cut to the quick. Not that he would have none of it; only that there were obvious blind spots in my reasoning. Unless it was fully automatic and closed to new material, CI could never 'run itself.' Its so-called 'minders,' the watchers, would always manipulate its users and content. Reality, no matter how devalued and miserable, was here to stay. With the rationing of sleep and a general embargo on natural fantasy, there would be no daydreams worth mentioning, hence no revolt against government abuses to control or even phase out CI – leaving it with a power that the authoritarian regimes of the past certainly never dreamt of. This was proof enough to Chevauchet that wilful delusion was winning out over the principle of reality. For him, this principle was non-negotiable.

'The scotomization of vision is already far along.' As harsh as I found his diagnosis, it was just. On this point, I would soon come to see eye to eye.

Chapter Eighteen

Despite at all times looking and sounding ambassadorial, and trying by peaceful means to retard the progress of CI, Chevauchet was powerless to stop something whose global appeal was so eyely. He could not himself sabotage the program; for one thing, he lacked the necessary skills.

For a while, he had collaborators who took inspiration from 'Le Passe-muraille,' as they nicknamed him. In the wake of their infrastructure attacks, some groups on CI noticed a significant drop in quality and complained that it was 'not as advertised' (language that betrayed they still believed themselves consumers, who had a choice to go elsewhere, or even opt out). A thorough investigation turned up nothing: no technical failures or rogue activity were detected. But, one by one, the collaborators turned away from the 'Passer-through-Walls' and, spellbound by CI, dropped like flies.

More alarming was the fact that, because the illusion of CI was so complete and seductive, these early collaborators preferred the state of wakefulness, ignoring the interdependence between daydreaming and sleep. Yet for his diplomacy to bear fruit, Chevauchet needed stakes in all three: dream, sleep, and reverie. This work did not consist in 'dream interpretation' or 'analysis.' First, he promoted Onirica by showcasing its virtues and clearing up common fallacies. Thus, Onirica was not 'the royal road' to anything, the privileged means and most direct route to 'real' desires that had been repressed. It was just the place where the creative imagination had the fewest restrictions. Without dreams' power to transform experience, reveries would always risk collapsing into that from which, by default, they did their high dive – the hard springboard of the real they found deficient. But daydreams did not simply take their cue from night-dreams. Instead, they complemented them (the best in them, ideally), contributing to that dimension of reality unique to oneiric experience.

I admit I struggled with Chevauchet's notion of dream-reality before fully grasping the nature of dream states. For a start, he disliked the opposition of dreams, whether night or day, to consciousness. As a matter of fact, he believed both kinds of dream to be integral to conscious experience. 'Normal,' that is to say, passive, waking consciousness, which registered an 'objective,' hard reality (existing outside and independently), to which it bound itself, was a scientific abstraction, an unproven hypothesis. If dreams prevailed over that waking reality by banding together, as they did in some hypersensitive individuals, they would activate a qualitatively different, 'deviant' consciousness, within which reality itself would be alterable.

It was thus elemental to defend the *right to dream* – a basic, natural, universal, inalienable right and freedom, nowhere explicit, and whose legal protection would be contrary to it, creating what is called a productive contradiction. As things stood, there was no sign of this happening. The boundless freedom to daydream was taken for granted (and when it came to night-dreams, few cared anymore). Its *actual* restriction, already far advanced, escaped notice. When something proliferated as much as dreams on the CI platform, fighting for the right to dream seemed like a waste of time. Why fight for what everyone, or nearly everyone, already had in abundance? No one appeared to realize that this piece of psychedelic engineering, this sham proliferation, had as its end goal dreaming's real extinction. Lulled by CI, none would awaken to legally secure dreaming as a right before it was gone – unless, at the last minute, it somehow became valued as essential, rather than as luxury. Chevauchet's plan to build an alternative network and community of dreamers to overtake CI was a race against time.

Chapter Nineteen

The values and ideals of Chevauchet belonged to a long underground history of opposition to the modern state. Among his many heroes were La Boétie, Pierre Leroux, Joseph Déjacque, Marx, Blanqui, Emma Goldman, and Louise Michel. Their writings were, in his words, 'jailbirds' tunnels beneath the imperial edifice.' In the years leading up to his mission, the state had become all-present, and all but invisible. There was broad consensus that we had finally entered the Cosmopolitan Age, the age of the universal state: Greater America, whose power, despite reaching across the globe, was 'diffuse,' 'fluid,' 'soft,' and 'harmless.' The unification of all nations under a single democratic government sounded to all ears like a dream come true, and one dared not question it, let alone name its totalitarian face. For all intents and purposes, there were no 'oppressed peoples' on the planet.

Onirica had, since time immemorial, been at least as global and sovereign a state, if of a different order. Looked at one way, it was still part of Greater America, provided that the latter was not under an *egeirocracy*, or a regime of total wakefulness (a permanent *state of exception* of sorts). Looked at from another angle, and more politically, it was an 'inland island,' a conspiratorial deep state undermining a world government hostile to it.

Until recently, everyone who frequented Onirica would do so once a day, ensuring the balance of power. This system of dual and overlapping statehood functioned seamlessly; power over minds was shared. Prolonged stays in Onirica – more than twelve hours – were rare and authorized only for the poor, the infirm, and the very young. No one was made to live in it permanently, though being spirited away there against one's will did happen. The same could not be said of the waking state, with which Greater America was synonymous and wanted to be identical. Of late, it had aggressively promoted abductions and exclusivity to weaken somnolence. It exercised its will to domination just short of declaring war.

As the waking world's human population swelled, Onirica's dwindled. This decline, not steep, was about to become a precipice. Extending over decades, it would terminate overnight – with the full-on assault on sleep. Sometimes, it is true, Onirica was black with people, bedded down, catching up on it, 'recharging their batteries.' But this was merely an epiphenomenon in a downward spiral, and soon many were getting their last fill of a 'good night's rest.' They felt they would be happier, more fulfilled, going without sleep altogether in exchange for working even longer hours, punctuated by sessions inside CI.

There was, however, an important difference in citizenship between the two states. The Onirican republic received both humans and animals. Animals dreamt – their dreams feebler and free-floating, to be sure, but also happier, or so Chevauchet maintained.

The Onirican embassy, its location in daydreams on the fringes of reality, was a strange, outré place. The founding fathers of Greater America did not suspect its presence, though they recognized the threat posed by spontaneous reverie. They increasingly stigmatized such wishful thinking as inefficient, wasteful, unhealthy, indulgent, inferior, and degenerate; as child's play, and nothing compared to the wonders of CI – the latter ostensibly providing a 'safe' outlet for it and, before long, a medium of its censorship.

The masterminds of CI sought by degrees to replace all natural creative imagination with artifice. They claimed it was for the sake of quality control: optimized content and better use of time, what with advances in the temporal compression of daydream experience. In reality, it was to abolish mental activity that was off the grid and went untracked. CI was a step up from what 'circuses' were for the Romans, appeasing the masses by spectacular diversions. To the extent that, for the time being, participation was still voluntary, it did not reek of total control. No one would accuse its makers of wilfully spreading political apathy.

Similarly, no one would credit Chevauchet's prediction that CI was temporary; that, once everyone bought into it, total control would be secured and followed by the interface's deactivation; that, having bankrupted the imagination, the ersatz would be retired. It was a preposterous idea when one thought of it. Crying wolf, is all. As for the death of the imagination, its poverty now manifest, would anyone truly mourn it?

'Why has natural imagination become undesirable?' I asked, artlessly. The reply – his most inspired to date – put everything in perspective:

'People usually associate creativity with works of art. But what is the occasional artwork alongside the creative energy displayed by everyone countless times a day? What is a David or a Van Gogh beside seething unsatisfied desires, daydreams in search of a foothold in reality, ideas, and gestures presaging nameless upheavals? The energies expended on artistic spectacles – like the interactive virtual mass theatre of CI – are energies diverted from the arsenal of individual reveries, which agitate against reality. Once armed and animated by the will to change the world – anything less would not be worth the trouble – there is no more question of treating them as fantasies.

'Daydreaming is directly subversive. Sometimes its subversion is spontaneous play, sometimes it is turning the master's tools against him, sometimes it is original creation. In all three cases it is subjective subversion or *détournement*. That is, it may be as unstructured, or as derivative, reflexive and reactive, or, again, as controlled and laborious, as you want, requiring no thought and attention or, to the contrary, a good deal of it. But it needs to have a basis in reality to gain any purchase on it. Daydreams are turned away from reality only in part. They are *reality without principle*. But no matter how unprincipled, they are real nonetheless.'

What made the imagination politically threatening was this radical subjectivity trained by natural, unassisted daydreaming.

'Strengthening the subjective core,' Chevauchet explained, 'is no easy matter. In the mind of each human being there is a hidden chamber, to which only reverie can find the door. A magic circle in which the world and the self are reconciled, where every childish wish comes true. The passions flower there: brilliant, poisonous blossoms wide open to the mood of the moment.

'Technology, falsely promising utopia, wants to bar the road to it, and by the same token suppress the purely magical aspect of the daydream. Even without any help from technology, it is by no means impossible for me to give objective form to everything I have ever dreamt of being. Surely everyone, at least once in their life, has been a little like a Charles Lassailly, a frenetic romantic, or like a Sergey Nechayev, that catechetical revolutionary. Lassailly, passing himself off as the author of a book he had never written, wound up as a true writer. And Nechayev, who began by cheating money out of Bakunin in the name of a non-existent terrorist organisation, later became the guiding light of an authentic group of nihilists. We all dream of passing through the eye of a needle, and some of us even manage it.'

The power of subjectivity, if only it could be harnessed and collectively expressed, was infinite. All seemed to turn for Chevauchet on nature, the imperative of following it. In his reaction to the persecution of natural desires and the concomitant cult of technology, I immediately saw a danger that was no less real for being hidden from him. This danger – his own blind spot, for a change – was fetishizing nature, making an idol of it, placing on it demands that it could never fulfill.

Chapter Twenty

Many of Chevauchet's 'teachings' were difficult to take in large drafts. Nor did he bother to sweeten them. But, in his tireless animation, he would sometimes shift from the often dry, critical register to something like poetry. He was at his most enthusiastic and least prosaic when speaking of reveries. His most memorable and whimsical turns of phrase were reserved for their praise.

Nocturnal dreams were 'pilgrimages to the underworld.' Reveries were 'flights.' This meant that night-dreamers contented themselves with oneiric tunnels opening right in front of them. The equivalent for daydreamers were utopian horizons.

Reverie became somnolence, somnolence reverie. Daydreams could easily pass or slide into night-dreams, and vice versa, when relished in a hypnagogic state. A dream of sexual fulfillment, for instance, could furnish a similarly themed daydream.

Transition in one direction, from reverie to dream, was marked by a 'prolapse,' or a fall downward. This was because the nocturnal dream had more 'gravity' as a self-contained world. Things found in it were 'dream-real.'

Reverie, meanwhile, was the reverse, a 'fall *upward*.' Neither fall was fatal, but they exposed the 'eggshell structure of so-called normal consciousness.'

Yet, for all their overlap, the two sorts of imagination remained irreducible to one another. The night-dream seemed to me to have no dreamer in it, as though there were no *cogito* there, no organizing consciousness. And yet some dreams were quite lucid. They created a sense of being simultaneously inside and outside looking in: both dreaming and daydreaming, asleep and awake.

Dreams and reveries were thus mutually permeable, intruding upon each other. Daydreams succumbed to the weight of sleep, to the gravity of their 'night doubles,' by hitting 'air pockets.' Conversely, absorbing them could lift certain oneiric moments, turbulent and convulsive, to where 'dreams levitated.'

And where, toward what regions, did they levitate? The 'beauty, truth, and goodness' of pure reverie. Night-dreams took on a higher coherence thanks to its poetic power. They grew wings and took to the air. When this happened and they united, dreams expanded consciousness.

In contrast to a night-dream, a reverie could not be recounted. But as it reached poetic heights, it lent itself to words and images, unique systems of inscription and depiction tantamount to poetic creation. There reverie 'played out its true destiny': it became beautiful. If a daydreamer had 'the gift,' they would turn their reverie into a work of art.

'Reverie is commonly classified among the phenomena of psychic détente,' said Chevauchet, making a fine point. 'It is lived out in a relaxed time which has no linking force. Since it functions with inattention, it is often without memory. It is a flight attached to the real as a kite is to the hand of a child. Under normal conditions, it does not yield an alternative reality. The horizon cast by it is thus not a world unto itself, even when inconsistent with the way things are for the daydreamer. But neither is such a horizon merely an extrapolation from the real. Although they are more tethered to reality than night-dreams, reveries are freer.'

By following 'the arc of reverie' – its strange, contradictory trajectory – waking consciousness, light as a feather, relaxed and floated. It 'clouded over,' and could be profoundly altered. The benefits were innumerable.

'Happiness is an idea that has not aged well,' he mused. 'Reverie comes to its rescue: It models well-being and puts it back on the map. The daydreamer and their reverie enter totally into the substance of felicity. You must tell whoever wants to be happy to begin by daydreaming well. This door to happiness stands open to everyone: building castles in the air, *châteaux en Espagne,* costs nothing!'

'But all this costs time, and time is valuable,' I objected. 'The living body must be fed. And isn't the policy precisely to universalize reverie? Wasn't CI meant to buy us time?' I was dismissed with a wave of the hand, like someone who had clearly not reflected on the matter from all possible sides.

'Nihilominus, nihilominus,' was his answer to me on this and similar occasions, to indicate that my point was moot and his firmly standing. He frequently cited reverie's 'irreality function' as useful in keeping at bay 'the hostile and foreign world in all its brutality.' By 'reverie' he meant, of course, the true and salutary, not the false, bastardized, CI kind. Without reverie, there was anguish, hopelessness, ennui, and misery. And when, ravaged by them, the mind fell apart, the body would soon follow.

Daydreaming was no less a gateway to happiness for being solitary. 'In this solitude, memories arrange themselves in tableaux that can accommodate anyone. Decor takes precedence over drama. Sad memories take on at least the peace of melancholy. Happy moments return and are embellished, irradiated by a feeling of well-being.

'And that is another difference between night-dream and reverie. The dream remains overloaded with the individual's badly lived daytime passions. Solitude becomes equivalent to hostility. It is strange and uncanny. It isn't quite *one's own* solitude, but something more generic. And when this solitude gravitates toward the muted, the suppressed, and the censored, the result is nightmares.'

The daydreamer's fantasy, on the other hand, linked by a myriad filaments the deepest layers of the unconscious with the highest products of human consciousness, which is to say, with works of art. It reconnected 'on its own terms' the night-dream to reality. And, most crucially, it preserved the collective and individual memory of freedom.

Fantasy as a distinct mental process was born and at the same time abandoned as soon as pleasure became subordinated to the principle of reality. Daydreaming appeared lax, untrue, and useless once reason prevailed, exacting, correct, and useful. It became 'mere' play, dismissed as what it always was: indeterminate, ubiquitous, and mutable. Indulgence in it became a source of shame, refraining from it a source of pride. But any such triumph over oneself was satisfying;

there was no real defence against pleasure. And if it could not be beaten, pleasure might as well be accepted. Not only could it then be managed, but also infinitely degraded.

From pleasure it is but a short step to reverie. As such, and even when out of practice, daydreaming continued to speak the language of the pleasure principle, of freedom from repression, of the gratification of uninhibited desire. But reality fell into place and proceeded according to the laws of reason, hostile to the language of reverie. Nevertheless, fantasy retained the structure and tendencies of the psyche prior to its organization for reality, prior to it becoming individual, set apart from other individuals. And by the same token, its creative imagination preserved the memory of the subhistorical, of a time 'when the life of the individual was the life of the genus and of the species, the image of the immediate unity between the universal and the particular under the rule of the pleasure principle.' In contrast, 'the entire subsequent history of man is characterized by the destruction of this *original unity*.' 'Original unity' was Chevauchet's magic charm, the universal formula.

Chapter Twenty-One

A pond can look bottomless when its surface reflects a sun or a sky. It seems all surface, with no suggestion of space below. Only evening reveals its depth. The sun, sinking, peels off the surface and leaves it black, an endless hole.

But to me all ponds and lakes looked alike, regardless of the impression they made as the day ran its course. They possessed at once their fragile sheet of glass – the same vitreous film, crystal-clear and paper-thin – and a profundity that was stronger than a mere suggestion. Like some mountain lakes, which, the higher up they are and the more perfectly they reflect the surrounding nature and clouds, the wider they open my eyes onto the abyss, as if by cutting away the cilia, the lids. Naked, circumscribed surface over seemingly infinite depth, and in this much like an eye – the eye being the image of a pond in the human head, not vice versa.

Since my new friendship, my time alone became rarer and rarer, though I cherished it. My thoughts gained in clarity what they lost in complexity, as they glided in aleatory fashion and would sometimes slow down so completely as to put me in mind of a snow-white swan floating upon still water.

One warm October day, Chevauchet seemed positively starry-eyed. We met, as usual, by the pond in the park.

'I still have much to show you,' he said. 'The part of Greater America where we built the embassy.'

It was a moment I had been waiting for, and I followed willingly, preferring an experiential outing to yet another lecture, however enlightening. Now that I had all the theory, I was interested in its application. I had blazed trails with him through the dark wood of nocturnal imaginings, and saw many that were in use. But the community of dreamers he envisioned, and on which he pinned his hopes, eluded me.

We circled around the lake. To think that I had been this way so many times and never before noticed the faun sculpted on the side of a boulder as if clambering up it, with a grimace and fearful glance cast downward over his shoulder, fleeing something. The park had an underground history, constructed as it was over horse shambles and a wasteland of old gypsum quarries, used to make plaster of Paris.

We passed the Carrefour de la Colonne, where several paths met, and where of the statue of a shepherd in pursuit of a wolf only the pedestal was left. It had been melted down during the last war for cannons to the occupying forces, along with *The Glaneuse*, a female gleaner inside the parkette at La Chapelle, the sculpture *Illusions and Regret* in the Gambetta Quarter, and the Place Clichy's statue of Charles Fourier. They were never restored.

'When all that's left is mythical fear and empty pedestals,' wondered Chevauchet, more to himself than to me, 'who will chase away the wolves?'

We exited the park and walked up Tunnel Street – a close enough pass – which rose and then dipped down as one hiked toward the Buttes and imagined that a seashore lay just the other side of this hump-of-a-beached-whale-of-a-hill.

We then took the Avenue of the Seventh Art, its name a nod to Ricciotto Canudo, a champion of cinema, and to the Studios Gaumont, once the largest in the world, which produced such silent gems as *Fantômas* and *The Château of Cards* at a time when Hollywood was still a citrus grove. Leaving the Combat Quarter, we proceeded down Rue des Solitaires, a street of which Chevauchet seemed particularly fond, and whose narrowness indeed favoured solitary walkers. We wound our way through the Villa du Progrès to the convergence of the streets Equality, Fraternity, and Liberty, where they begin or end. Here the neighbourhood no longer resembled postcard Paris or even the rest of the Quartier d'Amérique in which we now found ourselves, but a provincial town or a village. We chose Rue de la Fraternité and, eventually turning left, came to the entrance to the Hameau du Danube, or Danube Hamlet, a proto-gated community, apparently a relic of the English 1920s garden-city movement, itself inspired by turn-of-the-century utopian socialism. Access here was restricted to residents, but we managed to sneak in anyway and ambled unnoticed along wet cobblestones, admiring the architecture.

It would be difficult, Chevauchet pointed out, to find a residential complex with greater density of reference to the revolutionary-utopian past. But from the ensuing silence I guessed something was amiss, which had to do with the fact that a city so proud of this history preferred it imparted by street names and untold plaques. Most of the Hamlet's houses had been attractively modernized, sacrificing the original rusticity.

'Shameful!' he exclaimed finally. I had never seen him so agitated. 'They chip away at the place as though it had been left unfinished! The original idea is perfectly lost on them. They are wrecking a living museum. And for what? For their own damn convenience. They live only for themselves. Oh, they dream all right: they fantasize about better jobs, better cars, better vacations. Not better lives. A better life is not just the sum of its parts!

'Come, we'd best be on our way. We won't find any dreamers of promise here, not anymore.' And he gestured for us to go.

Chapter Twenty-Two

We ended up at a pleasant bar, where light drugs were traded, and the clientele, neither cool nor all that young, was less distracted, practised in medicating the profound. The alchemy of the place was such that one's sense of time was suspended, regardless of what music was playing, what one had taken, whether or not one was high, and whether the door was closed or open. This ambiance had everything to do with its name: le Rêve, the Dream.

We sat down for a drink and chatted with the current owner, 'The Headless Woman' (in tribute to Max Ernst), and none of it seemed quite real.

'That's what brings them here,' she laughed, when I mentioned the effect her café had on me. 'It's long been a favourite with writers, you know. They flock here to daydream. To escape reality. And I'm happy to help.'

I asked how long the Dream had been around.

'Oh, hard to say. It's the kind of factual question I rarely get,' she added, winking. 'My guess is at least since the end of the last war.'

I asked Chevauchet to describe to me what the other customers were fantasizing about. To my surprise, he did not invite me to see for myself, as he did with dreams. He said they were cosmic reveries, of the type that are tricky to access and impossible to narrate – a state of mind at once profoundly solitary, asocial, and outside time, what the Neoplatonists called *melancholia mentalis*. I gave the washed-out faces around me the once-over, and since they betrayed nothing of the sort, I had no choice but to take him at his word. So, the gap between the ideal and what existed made one melancholy ... Sensing my skepticism, Chevauchet assured me this was one of the last communal spaces where daydreams could be hatched like plots against reality.

The first of their kind had been the legendary Black Cat, le Chat noir. But the problem was that its two facets – the masonic and the aesthetic – which had gone international, did not communicate and collaborate. The diplomacy of the masons was completely obscure to the artistic youth that gathered there to stage their shadow plays. What the first conspired in spirit, the second should have vested in symbolic spectacle appealing to the senses. Obviously, neither masons nor artists – a.k.a. dreamers and daydreamers – alone could stage a revolution; only the two together.

'It is a little-known fact,' continued Chevauchet, 'that the Black Cat was initially the Black Swan, in memory of 1789. The French Revolution – the original one – was like the "black swan" of the philosophers: something that had been thought impossible, inconceivable even, until it manifested itself, shaking the foundations of historical understanding, putting almost everything into question. This question mark needed a name, and since its shape was a bit like a swan (a *cygne*, being in French a homonym for "sign"), even though they had never seen one like it (for its feathers were black), they felt compelled to call it a swan, and to accept that there were things beyond their ken that might yet come to pass and topple the old order, washing away what were hitherto certainties. That was the perceived effect of the Revolution, irrespective of whether you were for or against it. The assumption until then was that all popular risings were revolts. And revolts, like rebellions, insurgencies, and such, could be contained and put down. What happened, however, exceeded all expectations, except those that were mad, the brainchildren of visionaries.

'Alas, a black swan was heavier, more fatidic, than a black cat. That made it less suited as the name of a nightclub that was all about making light. So, in the end, they decided against it and went with le Chat noir. And they never got up to anything beyond mischief. All because an old occult emblem found by Fulcanelli in a certain château and familiar to the rich patrons of the future cabaret cast the swan as a suicidal creature. *Propriis pereo pennis,* I die by my own feathers, if I am not mistaken, was the emblem's motto – a veritable swan song, as the bird's neck is pierced by an arrow fletched with its own plumes. They did not much like the association. It was worse than bad luck. Like shooting yourself in the foot, since feathers are not for killing but for flying, and for writing. Anyway, compared to a popular superstition, it was too recherché.'

Chapter Twenty-Three

We headed north, and on the way passed the Museum of Eroticism, which was closing its doors. Its dissolution proved that Paris was changing. Many of the *objets* on display scrupulously catalogued for auction had not sold. These circumstances turned the place into a museum of itself. On a whim, moved by nostalgia more than sexual curiosity, I proposed that we step inside, even if the daydreams evoked in us, tardy visitors, could only be predictable and uninspired. But I was to be proven wrong.

Coming from all four corners of the world, the exhibition's remnants were of a bewildering variety, the ancient pressed against the modern, the tawdry beside the tastefully fake, the serious touching the humorous, the exuberant tickling the deadpan – there being truly something for everyone, from the happy-go-lucky tourist to the most discerning amateur. I particularly liked a miniature coffin made of wood, whose cover, when slid aside, revealed the expected skeleton. But as one proceeded to remove the lid, his erect member popped up suddenly. I recalled seeing another toy of this kind: the figurine of a priest, his chasuble shrouding the same gross indecency.

I was not the only one fond of the obscene little coffin; an old woman stood next to me eyeing it as well. She liked the way the object provided, in the form of a toy, a synthesis of life and death that was light, lowbrow, and unpretentious. It was a pity that its surprise would soon consign it to oblivion or a private curiosity cabinet, and that the associations it aroused directly, regardless of its maker's intention, would hereafter be available only in roundabout, high and heavy fashion, out of the way of many who could appreciate its unsubtlety, which was more to their taste.

The most beautiful and titillating work in the collection was surely a very large painting on wood of an angel visiting Teresa of Ávila, whose pale habit resembled a great unmade bed. It was a mechanical object, its mechanism broken. The sole moving part, also the sole piece of flesh visible below the saint's face, in the picture's bottom half, was her foot, which, pink and dainty, ever so slightly undulated. The painting drew inspiration from her ecstatic vision, in which an angel had pierced her with a flaming sword, then withdrew it along with her entrails. The creature stood smiling above, speckled with blood, with one hand raising the sheets covering her breast, with the other flashing its gold 'arrow.'

The decommissioned museum seemed to stand for the general state of the entire strip between Clichy and Pigalle. The adult cinemas and sex shops with live window displays – it was all on the verge of going down history's great drain, to join the official brothels or *maisons closes*, the catch-as-catch-can halls, and the cabaret-haunts – Heaven, Nothingness, Hell (Le Ciel, Le Néant, L'Enfer). Gone were the 'spaces of sleep,' as these last were known back in the day, when

Montmartre was still a hotbed of revolution; vanished their macabre illusions and phantasmagorias, the coffin tables and chandelier of skull and bones, to which laughter and song had been the living accompaniment. It was there that young poets held nightly hypnotic séances of oracular group 'slumber' in a prelude to Surrealism.

The artists were mostly gone now, the idling transvestites, too, came and went, and only the odd African marabout still handed out to passersby his promise of healing, love, and success. The lurid Paris of old, hardly a trace of which remained, had to be taken on faith. The souls we passed were conscious of the surrounding obsolescence. Their reveries mourned the *genius loci,* which at one time solicited the free expression of desire and sexual liberty. Without it, they felt at sea, yet unfree.

Chapter Twenty-Four

Next, Chevauchet took me by Rue du Temps perdu, the street of Lost Time, which, by then, existed only in the memory of some sentimentalists. He seemed deflated by the fact that, in those few who still remembered it, the place provoked regret: to think of all the time lost to daydreaming!

Chapter Twenty-Five

We carried on. It was only a matter of time, Chevauchet said, before we came across someone with oppositional leanings, whose fantasies were the targeted projectiles he was after. He sought 'a true poet,' with dreams that were mobilizing, communicable, who brashly proclaimed, 'I live my dream as reality!'

It had crossed my mind previously that the door through which poets passed was one whereby a psychopath could easily enter. They had been known to keep company. But I kept such thoughts to myself, wary of crossing him.

We were heading down what was formerly Rue des Maléfices, one of the most garish zones in the city, vandalized and defaced by graffiti, spiced with urine and excrement. After the closure of the university, the area became home to the Anarchabêtes, a sect of petty thieves and rebel poets – anarchists – who squatted the site of the bookshop Shakespeare & Company, and who, like other partisans of *anarcho-mutisme* – when they were not speaking in tongues, babbling under the influence – communicated exclusively by manual signs.

The season was changing again. We passed a pair of sphinxes, hailing from warmer climes, drafted here by orientalist whimsy to pose as terrestrial gargoyles that, chilled to their stony core, vomited water all day long. They adorned an old fountain to Napoleon – a hero of wakefulness, having famously economized on sleep.

Nearby, in one of the covered passages, a little boy stopped to window-gaze. Attracted by mere craving but detained by a dream, he stared longingly at the pretty boxes of exotic chocolate, which had the power once held by postage stamps to take one on faraway voyages.

Chapter Twenty-Six

The early-morning mist scattered as we crossed the Seine via the Île Saint-Louis, our stepping stone. We turned left immediately thereafter, walking some distance to the southeast, before drawing up, at Chevauchet's bidding, at the middle of a city block. I looked up. Barely noticeable above an unexceptional doorway and styled in classical Latin capitals were the words *ARENAS OF LUTETIA*.

Several steps into the courtyard put us inside an oval amphitheatre, and we made for the seating area, only a section of which survives. It was the idea of calm. We were alone but for one other person, their gender indeterminate, sitting in a great coat twenty paces away and watching the sunny arena like a harbour, asquint. I looked out as well and saw the sand where gladiators used to cross swords turn moist and the basin fill up with water. Some moments later, two ships blew in, shaking out their sails like immense wings, their long masts quivering and dark oars paddling like the webbed feet of a swimming bird. They were flanked by a flotilla of smaller, less muscular vessels. These, too, were armed, and presently the naumachia began. But the crews manning them, wearing fierce expressions, were too large for the naval battle to look convincing. The more earnestly they sought to imitate reality, the more outlandish the show seemed. And I could not help thinking that, given their basic disproportion, the illusion would have worked better as farce – rather than straining for a spectacle of the first order.

My mind gradually strayed from the ludicrous skirmish likely conceived by our neighbour. The water, instead of giving me a shimmering Fata Morgana of my own to play with, bathed the ships in reflected light, occasioning a reverie in which they were real swans, craning their necks as they took the measure of their enormous wingspan. White, they wore their black markings like visors.

Chevauchet's face – when, taking my eyes off my swans for an instant, I turned toward him – showed displeasure. Nothing of what we had conjured transcended gratuitous fancy, indulged for the sake of amusement. Summoning the lacklustre image of a historic event in miniature and of two swans mating – neither was a dream of beauty that bore the promise of happiness.

But as I went back to imagining the birds, so majestic, and yet, in their courtship, so graceless, in this Gallic theatre, discovered and preserved centuries later in 'the capital of modernity,' the voice of a poet called to me from a less distant past:

Old Paris is no more (the form of a city
Changes more quickly, alas! than a mortal's heart)

They were Baudelaire's swans I saw, escaped from their cage – a sign! His verses had come to life on their own, as my mind, dreaming, confirmed the truth of their sentiment.

There was nothing concrete about my reverie, nothing definite. Yet I desired with all my heart to dwell in it, and in the layers of the city that induced it, as they had *Les Fleurs du mal*. I had scarcely left the sleepy arena when another poet, Jean Paulhan, enjoined me from a plaque with still loftier words:

> *Passerby who come before this, the first monument of Paris, imagine that the city of the past is also the city of the future and that of your hopes!*

I tried as best I could to communicate to Chevauchet my fleeting impressions. Though he was still visibly disappointed in me, he conceded they may have been beautiful. The thing was, they were wholly devoid of volition.

'Poetic fantasies,' he said, 'be they the most melancholy, take us only so far, and no further. They leave us dissatisfied. There is something missing. Trying to lay hold of it, we rally. And that is only as it should be.'

He had joked, recently, that a diplomat's bed was big enough for two. For the first time since our meeting, I sensed I had let him down, which implied he had plans for me. I felt personally responsible, as though I had neglected my duties, was not doing *what had to be done*.

Chapter Twenty-Seven

Threading through waking dreams differed in many respects from dream-hopping. Night-dreams were diversions for sleep, escapes from darkness. Daydreams, as vain hopes, chimeras, distractions in a waking state, were resistances to attention, absences from the day. Their fully fledged form put them closer to frenzy or lunacy than to the meditative activity they had come to designate. They proved, at any rate, thinner, less visually creative, and more ephemeral when dreamt than did night-dreams. It was impossible to find a foothold in them. One did not have the experience of penetrating a self-contained world, but of being carried some distance on the powerful wings of strange desires or suddenly shot through with them. Rather than letting us pass, as we did through dreams, they passed through us or lifted us, at the unhurried pace that is theirs. Their tenor (if I can call it that), even when melancholy, was typically positive and associative, so that one did not lose one's bearings as in oneiric states. Most important of all, they were overwhelmly pleasant, far sweeter than dreams, and too often made up of images their subject found gratifying, such as figurations of harmony and delight. On that basis alone, they were more agreeable to experience second-hand.

All of these generalizations were true enough, but even from my limited exposure there were other, more pertinent conclusions to be drawn. Chevauchet seemed out of touch with the actual direction most reveries were taking. When imagining fulfilled wishes, for example, they were no longer adventurous but conservative. When concerning projects, they were not boldly spinning their future but cocooning and protective. Many were simply too self-absorbed to sustain the hopes Chevauchet placed in them. Yet he remained convinced that these were exceptions, or at least in the minority, and that we had merely caught them at a bad time. He had no problem condemning such 'dreams dumped in a puddle,' of a feather with those from CI.

Meanwhile, he himself, it struck me, dreamt with blind conviction and ever greater urgency of reveries of which there was little evidence: reveries that were noble and other-centred. As he fantasized changing the world based on them, the tip of my tongue balanced only one word, which it did not let fall: la-la land. There was something about Chevauchet's idea of community that could keep him going forever, notwithstanding evidence to the contrary. This was the quixotic quest for a solution: the one, elusive fantasy that, truly selfless, would be just, and universally claimable; a rara avis; a great exception, where all noble human dreams came together and whose content could never be qualified. If only it were found, all the sleepless, white nights, all the tossing and turning, all the nightmarish visions that haunt dreamland would be made good at last.

Chapter Twenty-Eight

That day we made one final stop, on the grounds of the Hôpital Sainte-Anne. Chevauchet revealed he had high hopes for the reveries of the mad – a turn in his thinking so of a piece I should have anticipated it.

'There are great artists among them,' he confided, 'great poets. They spend so much of their time sleeping and wandering aimlessly, their rational faculty dulled by medication. They pass fluidly between day- and night-dreams, from one into the other. The boundary generally so clear to us for them barely exists.'

We entered the hospital's grounds from Rue Cabanis and strolled up and down the leafless interior alleys. These were named after such luminaries as Maurice Ravel, Antonin Artaud, and Gérard de Nerval, not all of whom had spent time within its walls. City life was shut out of this parklike ensemble, creating an oasis of tranquility. The lawns were freshly trimmed, the roads and sidewalks spotless, and only those buildings whose facades were in need of cleaning showed signs of their age. The patient body was a mix of 'traditional' inmates, confined and incurable, and 'contemporary' habitués, in and out, as in a spa. For these reasons, one had the impression – more intense than almost anywhere else in Paris – of being in two or even three superposed historical periods simultaneously.

The modern mad – whose mystical fantasies (issuing as they did from dreariness and longing) had once pointed the way to happiness, to utopia, and cast an unforgiving light on the pedestrian, self-seeking lives of the sane – were mad no more. As a plaque put up by the hospital's PR team proudly stated, 'It is at Sainte-Anne that the first treatments for the gravest mental disorders were developed.' The words were a caption to the oracular ravings of Jeannot, a young peasant who, shortly before taking his own life, had etched them into the oak floor of his room. On permanent display for its historical value, his work stood as 'a testament to the gravity that these illnesses can have without care being adapted to the needs of the individual patient.'

The two patients whose path we crossed, and into whose thoughts we could tune, were perfectly in possession of their senses and feeling fully restored to the world. I was confirmed in my impression when, following in their footsteps, we came to a small subterranean gallery exhibiting artwork from the hospital's own collection. Art therapy, pioneered here, and for which Sainte-Anne had become renowned, continued to this day. But among the particular set of drawings, paintings, and scrolls on view, none was recent.

One piece especially caught my eye, for it seemed to encapsulate what was missing from this place where the ill no longer mingled with the lost. It was a small *croquis* – souvenir for a fellow patient presumably about to leave the premises. Dedicated to Monsieur Fouron by one René Ernest Bredier and dated September 1942, it showed a middle-aged man, fully dressed down to his slippers, reclined on his side, with one hand in his trouser pocket and the other tucked underneath his head, his eyelids drawn. In this pose, floating on the idea of a bed, the folds and shadows formed just so by his clothes and rendered faithfully in pencil, he resembled a shrivelled leaf fallen to the ground in early autumn.

Chapter Twenty-Nine

'Out of season!' was how Chevauchet described his work at the time, casting about for an explanation of his failure to get anywhere close to the utopian fusion he was seeking. He had observed once before of autumn that it was the best time of the year for diplomacy. In autumn, the light induced whole suites of reverie. As if to compensate for the impending loss of foliage, fall's 'riots of colour,' its unrecorded 'sonatas' and 'symphonies,' elevated the spirits and gave rise to a 'late' optimism.

Winter had been long, and he looked forward to spring. Even I could see the seasonal impediments to his mission. There was the lack of light, to begin with. Contrary to what might be thought, winter favoured not daydreams but dreams following one another in close succession over long stretches of sleep, delving so deeply, and so sunken in consequence, that our descent proved tricky, to say nothing of a plunge from a daydream, so vertiginous it took my breath away.

Winter, season of discontent. But I wanted to know what it was a season *for*. Chevauchet's replique was brief:

'Sleep and death. These days, mostly not sleep.'

Surely it had some other use, I insisted, some silver lining, and could be turned over for our purposes and the general good.

The other half of the problem, it then emerged, was the relentless cold. With geoengineering gone wrong, people were too preoccupied with keeping warm to relax and let their minds drift.

'One day it will get so cold that Hell itself will freeze over,' he stated, trying his utmost to sound both plausible and prophetic. 'You will see. They are cooling you down on purpose because they are doing it artificially.'

That afternoon, snow fell in spades. As if answering a challenge, it gave everything a thick fleece. Hard reality showed through where it was cleared or melted. The slickness of the asphalt, its glistening blackness by night, attracted victims with its solidity like a dark magnet. The fluffy white fairytale never lasted long. The snow-clad house, standing for comfort and happiness, provoked petty acts of vandalism. And through even a single broken window, the cold crept in, killing the dreamlife inside. There was no end in sight to the justified resentment with which the 'seasonally appropriate' freezing temperatures and grim hunger sabotaged the dreams of the poor, which contained the highest quotient of resistance.

'Another Little Ice Age could finish off their useless fancies,' quipped Chevauchet with dark irony.

Chapter Thirty

These fantasies of the poor, as rare and precious as they were in such bitter meteorology, Chevauchet thought anemic.

'They are entirely circumscribed by the realm of necessity: material needs, food, shelter, warmth. What have they to bind them to Onirica? Frayed and loose ends. Nothing but residue.'

There could be no doubt about it: he was close to despair. He saw (how rightly, I would soon know) the crackdown on sleep-time as the world's systematic and final disenchantment. With the new surveillance methods in place, he worried over what would become of Onirica, the embassy, and the entire mission if he should lose his ground. Dreamers who hosted him not long before were unavailable, and those who could be counted upon to remain asleep were now farther apart and fewer. He needed to know that he had always somewhere to land, another dreamer he could call on, a 'rendezvous' where he could appear should one of his long-standing hosts forego dreaming and, under pressure from the authorities, renounce sleep, cutting off Chevauchet's way home. *Brief* general awakenings did not pose a mortal threat to him; he could still tarry on the edges of consciousness until sleep again engrossed his host. But with the repressions against sleep intensifying, his life was in jeopardy, making difficult all dream diplomacy.

There were of course still dreamers he could depend on, such as me. He was my guest. I was reliable – this must be how he initially chose me, although we never discussed it. He must have known that sleeping was my 'keystone habit' and nothing could keep me from it, not even a gun pointed at my head. But he needed legion like me, as he needed space to operate, and the operation of coupling night- to daydreams was an exceedingly delicate one, tolerating no missteps.

'If worse came to worst, and there were no human dreamers left,' I asked naively, 'could not animals do the dreaming in our place?'

I imagined animals as so many seeders, sowing dreams in those lacking them.

But this was not a durable solution. The embassy, Chevauchet's outpost in reality, needed both dreamers and daydreamers. Animals – be they dogs, swans, or horses – were incapable of complex reverie and, in any case, should not have to do the work of men. They could not take over our responsibility.

As for infiltrating CI, my cautious suggestion, he would not hear of it.

Chevauchet's voice, I noticed, was growing raspier and weaker in its determination. At times, he would lose it completely. 'They want to kill off all the dreamers!' he croaked, and I did my best not to show the pity I felt toward him. His physique, too, seemed diminished. His coat hung loosely from his shoulders as if there were no substance filling it, the inside hollow like the cape of a ghost, a cavity for the wind to swirl leaves in. This I took as a sign less of exhaustion than of disillusionment – a serious malady that in him, who harboured all illusions, could prove fatal.

More and more, he muttered instead of addressing me, plaintive words not meant for my ears, questions left dangling – like 'At what price...?' which he for once succeeded in finishing: '...do you buy solidarity?' He was alluding, of course, to Greater America's union with Onirica, to its coming, ever-deferred transformation. So preoccupied was he by his para-worldly cares and rising complications (of which I still had only the slimmest conception) that he sometimes seemed light years away. Minutiae could worm their way into his mind and obscure the big picture, the gestalt, the synthesis. They were like the *petites perceptions* noted by Leibniz – tiny impressions and alterations of the soul, normally too minuscule, numerous, unvarying to notice – which, blown out of proportion somehow, coloured his entire vision, fixing themselves, in their obsessive return, in his memory.

He would remark, for instance, on the light in a room: 'Did you make a note of it, burning with poetic ecstasy? I hope so.' I did my best to keep up, but how could I? In the quaint stone house in which we stood, a lone oil lamp fought off the inner gloom. Any ecstasy it may have had was lost on me. 'Whenever I see a river in a dream,' he said on another occasion, 'I look for whether it flows, rough and brisk, like the foreground of a painting, or whether it is motionless, neat, unelaborate, tying the background like a ribbon, or maybe just a line of filiform silver, the mere suggestion of a river…' – differences so subtle they seemed to me wholly without consequence.

More traces of his own forgotten, unconscious states than objective indexes of another's individuality, such wee perceptions, the way he attended to and unfurled them, were a window on his peculiar sensibility and method. I began to imagine that every one of his passions and decisions could ultimately be traced to the things he found remarkable and singled out for reflection in the dreams of others, things of which their dreamers themselves were unaware. He once confessed to lacking an unconscious, vaunting his complete awareness and perfect memory – for precisely such things. He was self-transparent, 'leaping over my own shadow rather than jumping at it,' he boasted in jest. But I had my doubts. Not only were the effects of these perceptions on himself opaque to him, he did not even recognize their opacity. I further wondered if the small impressions he gleaned on his rounds were not perhaps of the same character and order of magnitude for their dreamers – and if, by his exaggerated attention to their dream expressions, he did not end up 'catching' and sharing them. Was it not owing to their existence and subliminal effects at every moment, I reasoned, that the present – waking, and perhaps dreamt as well – was at once perpetually charged with the past and big with the future, as Leibniz thought? Was this not, in fact, how every age, every epoch, 'dreamt the future,' as Chevauchet was fond of saying?

He wanted this future dreamt more directly. Dreaming it was supposed to both anticipate and bring it about – 'awaken' it. Elements of night- and daydreams would be realized in the course of our waking up. This business of awakening was no mere metaphor for mental vigilance; it was also literal and meant coming out of slumber. One opened a new pair of eyes, through which the world not only looked, but actually *was*, different.

This was indeed the nub of his doctrine, and its weakness. Dreams could not simply map out the future. They were unrealizable, since realization entailed imposing upon them the traditional, logical and physical, demands of rationality. It was bad faith pretending otherwise. Worse, to insist on awakening as the turning point, as the only way dreams were made good on, appeared, as time went on, complicit with the status quo – in a way that settling scores with it in dreams did not. To have commerce with 'normal' consciousness and action was to court compromise from an uneven footing. I suspected that, even in the best case, such a negotiated future could only be a letdown.

The leaven turning dreams into ascendants, or 'rising signs,' was *hope*.

'It is in its dreams,' he said, taking a fresh run at it, 'that society reflects its conditions of existence and expresses its desire to surmount the bad in them. But without hope, their "active principle," dreams are not enough to transform reality. The criticism of the status quo that is implicit or explicit in them needs activation.'

As he saw it, real action remained unfinished, and the revolutionary past, as a result, unfulfilled. Assuming there was still hope left, was there enough of it?

Chapter Thirty-One

He was nothing if not persistent, His Excellency Chevauchet. He kept at it. Given the setbacks and waning confidence in the success of his mission, his resolve and vitality often amazed me. I had been accompanying him daily on his travels for many months now. With each passing day, daydreams appeared to him more 'in their true light' – hopelessly compromised by the very fact of arising in a 'bad totality.' I myself had already remarked that the less time one had to night-dream, the more one-dimensional and threadbare became one's diurnal creations. Nocturnal dramas giving expression to repressed wishes and fears acted as a valve, releasing much of the pent-up eroticism and violence, and bypassing morality altogether. They conformed to the crude image Sigmund Freud cast of them. Without this outlet, natural daydreams (such as they were) risked being turned into vehicles for base desires, monopolized by sexual or even murderous fantasies in the breast. Nothing higher would germinate in them; nothing concerned with the world outside oneself or containing the seeds of a universe.

But there was something still more worrisome: the nether extension of voluntary servitude. The dreams we traversed practically demonstrated that freedom could be captured even in its last bastion. It was not merely that its symbols had changed; freedom no longer spoke through them.

Finally, there was the numbing effect of ubiquitous, 'universal' information. Here is how Chevauchet once illustrated it to me:

'One cannot dream of the most beautiful girl in the world in ignorance of who or where she might be. She has not gone unnoticed; she has already been identified; someone, some headhunter most likely, has already hunted her down for the cover of a magazine, already modelled her for a CI avatar, where she can be devoured, feeding the fantasies of millions upon millions.'

Information was spectacle, mass entertainment, a constant screen interposed between world and mind. It left nothing to the desiring imagination, since whatever was worth being shown was spectacularly overexposed and, no matter how sensual or luxurious to begin with, all but stripped of its aura – coming preconsumed and predigested in ways that often were unimaginative, trailing behind it virtually, like a tail there was no getting around. Why even make the effort to imagine anything for oneself? Who needed daydreams when one had virtuality?

The effect of virtual reality on the sales of luxury (superfluous) goods was not surprising. The switch over to virtuals, ever cheaper to produce, had been smoothed by CI and by a campaign marketing them as more environmentally friendly than the 'real thing.' Such sensory solicitation and oversaturation were lethal to daydreams that did not revolve around commodities.

'The death of imagination in ordinary women and men,' as Chevauchet liked to put it, was taking place before our very eyes. He even had a special word for it: *fantacide*.

Chapter Thirty-Two

Chevauchet never spoke about his past. It was always present for him, and if he could have it his way, it would always be autumn. I could not help wondering how long he had been around, if time indeed was applicable to his existence – as what I took to be his winding down suggested it was. How long ago did he appear, if appearance was indeed his mode of being? Was he an original, or did he have models, predecessors?

The little I learned of his origins was fascinating. He was born in 1939 in a Pyrenean village, a war child raised in hiding on account of his racial profile. This underground childhood, passed *en cachette,* determined his mistrust not only of authority but of hard reality, from which ever after he was in static flight: at first, a fugitive, to escape detection, and later, for refuge in the happiness of dreams.

The faraway war came to an end, yet the early experience of hiding and shelter, of moral clarity and political polarity, of having to distinguish enemy from friend, and an imagination that more than made up for his inability to pass the time reading, marked him forever. This *vita imaginativa* was not, he stressed, a 'limited life,' since his objective confines spurred him to push back against the limits of fantasy to compensate for the poverty of his everyday. He compared it to the effect of losing a sense like sight, the remaining senses finding ways to balance the loss by their own development. The only difference being that with the loss of physical freedom – not itself a sense but a midwife to the senses – one needed to compensate for all of them. Failing this adaptation, under such circumstances, life would have been impossible.

In the end, I knew next to nothing about Chevauchet's family and personal history. I did learn he had been married and had one child, and deeply regretted both. He thought the notion that one cared about the future of the world more if one had children, and the more one had of them, was patently false:

'The things we are willing to change and are exhorted to do for their sake, the social gains which may or may not, in turn, carry over to their children, are few and insignificant and often outweighed by the losses. We leave the world to them a greater mess than when we found it. We may make wiser lifestyle choices and model sociability and civility for a time. Few of us, however, are moved to pursue a righteous path to foster our children's sense of planetary responsibility. We must already have been set on such a path by destiny, and are likelier to step off it when a child enters the picture. After all, we are expected to think no sacrifice too great for it. There are, of course, exceptions – advocacy and philanthropy sparked by a child's handicap or by the experience of adoption. This should not blind us to the fact that when we project onto our children our unrealized dreams, which, incidentally, they are unlikely to fulfill, we absolve ourselves of the duty to take an active interest in the world, to intervene in it – we prefer to stay in our own little corner of living hell rather than attempt to change it. Our interest is, from then on, mediated through them, moderated by what is good for our child, whom we protect and monitor like a big investment rather than as a part of humanity. Parenthood, by focusing us narrowly, reinforces both capitalist and statist instincts – prosperity and security for a few, for the rest fear of poverty and anarchy. Our self-interest is thereby redoubled. I can find no good social reason, but only excuses, for reproducing. Better to have disciples than children.'

Shortly after May 1968, Chevauchet moved to Paris and started a publishing house to promote critical theorists and anarchist philosophers, both dead and living. I assumed he had his share of ideals and ambition. The experience of militant dreaming in those days prepared him for his 'succession,' as he called it, to the ambassadorial place.

'At any given time, there are at least two politically conscious Oniricans: the ambassador (mentor) and his successor in training. The man who would hand over the baton to me I met abroad, on a trip to Moscow. I was part of a French delegation invited by the underground independent labour union SMOT to meet Russian dissidents recently released from psychiatric hospitals and prisons. It was autumn 1988, perestroika, and we had hopes for unification with a realm of fantasy.

'On my last afternoon there, I struck out on my own on a walk to Neskuchny Sad, the oldest corner of the famous Gorky Park. Excited to see a foreigner (the giveaway being a francophone edition of the *Moscow News* I had purchased in the lobby of my hotel), a man struck up a conversation with me in fluent French. He was planning a “trip” – in other words, to defect – and wanted my telephone number, which I was only too happy to give him.

‘A week later, we saw each other again, this time in Paris. I asked if he had a place to stay. He said he was living in an embassy, and that it was not the Russian one. Travel restrictions allegedly did not apply to him: he could come and go as he pleased, and no one back home had so much as an inkling of his absence.

‘Kolnikov, for that was his name, was no ordinary dissident. He dropped enough hints. Luckily, he was not mistaken when he said I was “ambassador material,” ripe to represent Onirica. I hope I did not disappoint him. Come to think of it, you too would make a fine ambassador …

‘The rest, as they say, is history. Two years later to the day, in mid-November, a fever carried him away. He was so fired up by the Autumn of Nations, the events in Poland, Germany, China …’

As for me, I was growing accustomed to the drift of his ellipses.

Chapter Thirty-Three

The months of spring saw a slew of attacks on wishful thinking and the creative imagination. Their authors skewered every 'utopist' and 'visionary' known to history, no matter their politics. They took an axe to cinema, the 'dream factory,' and to poetry, 'the medium of prophecy,' denouncing their practitioners as charlatans pulling wool over people's eyes.

This genre of hatchet job was not new; oneirocriticism, already practised among the ancient Greeks and Islamic mystics, had become a fixture of intellectual life, under one name or another, in the nineteenth century. It had lost none of its popularity among modern reformists. But the extent to which the media had mainstreamed this brand of lettered butchery, and feasted on the meat of it, gave us cause for alarm. *Constructive* criticism of the 'dream-lefties,' the hated *oneiro-gauchistes* hostile to the status quo, was out of the question. The only acceptable way to comment now was damagingly and destructively. Another world was impossible. There were no alternatives. As long as you railed against the do-gooders and their air castles, or cried bloody murder while pointing to anarchists, naming names when necessary, you were guaranteed an avid audience.

I had been reading everything I could get my hands on of this literature to *learn the language of the enemy* (the maxim of she who had taught us, French schoolchildren, English). It was highly toxic writing, and, considering the nullity of its content, well executed. It called, in voices amplified with every iteration, in the dated idiom characteristic of these fanatical conservatives, for a new Prohibition. The cure for society's woes was to kick for good the 'opium of the masses.' But the tenor of the metaphor was not, as in the days of Marx and Lenin, religion. It dug deeper, much deeper, and came up with ... sleep.

Sleep was the source of all idleness; sleep was a drain on the economy; sleep induced illusions that competed with the demands and duties of reality; sleep enfeebled the will and was for the weak; sleep interfered with technical innovation, and with the swift completion of pressing public projects. In short, sleep was evil, and evil – sleep.

Bene dormit qui non sentit quam male dormiat: he sleeps well who feels not how ill he sleeps. Those for whom the few stolen minutes of slumber were a relief from oppression and the torture of overwork, and who were by no means a visible minority, had every right to feel threatened. The pamphlets denounced them as a 'menace,' 'melancholics,' 'spaniels,' 'dog-faced,' 'bags of bones,' and '*canaille*.' I could have sat down and written the primer for this novel *lingua imperii*. Insomnia was no longer 'voluntary' but 'recommended.' 'Closing one's eyes' became synonymous with 'conspiracy.'

Such perversions of language by the professed 'friends of the people' were as rife as their spread seemed unstoppable. And, as anyone else who followed the discourse sedulously could have predicted, by midsummer, insomnia went from 'recommended' to 'mandatory.' It was to usher in a 'great and full awakening' – physical, moral, spiritual, and of the 'dormant,' untapped faculties – an eye-opening available to everyone like Holy Communion (the religious overtones clearly calculated).

To prevent interference with this universal illumination, sleeping under any pretext, on any occasion, was outlawed – all for the 'greater good of society.' Selling people on insomnia took such duplicitous slogans as *One man who does not sleep makes two men, and two is always better than one*. These 'two-in-ones' were mechanical, their bodies relieved of organic torpor. Bodies ruled by their organs were abject and wretched; bodies controlling their vital functions were godlike, and saw their powers multiply. The mind, no longer stultified by sleep, underwent fission, unlocking its unused capacity. A world peopled by savants awaited!

All 'estates' – not just the elites – would get 'the boost,' a new drug called Potium, to partake of this beatific state of high-functioning sleeplessness. Yet the social structure was to be no better for it. A new hierarchy emerged. On the bottom, there were the underdogs, as you might expect. Higher up, the 'technicians' enjoyed a self-evident utility. Above them, finally, sat the 'specialists' – measly technocrats with significant, publicly defined administrative duties. With this new *nomenklatura* came a new nomenclature. The Minister of Education became 'Virtual Literacy Specialist.' The Ministry of the Interior now went by 'Specialty for the Maintenance of Public Order and Consciousness.' And the top brass of the ruling ASP, Alternative Socialist Party, hid behind the superlative 'Specialty of Specialties,' with the Office of Prime Minister (that holy of holies) predictably retitled 'Office of the Chief Specialist of Specialties.'

As for the 'Specialist of Occupations,' he scrapped the luxury of the thirty-five-hour workweek: the workers of the future could easily put in twenty hours per day, in several shifts, with breaks for three square meals. Downtime in any shape or form was frowned upon, and was on its way out. *Freedom through work! Work liberates!* – these mottoes were only vaguely familiar, and chanting them with an upbeat air was enough to make them contagious. Gainful employment was, of course, not guaranteed. Productivity, we were assured, did not need remuneration to 'count' in the eyes of 'leaders of industry.'

Offenders against the system – a label earned for the smallest infraction – were punished with (unmedicated) sleep deprivation. The daily Potium fix was withheld from them.

Over the weeks in which these 'final touches' were rolled out by our 'specialists without spirit' – gradually and as inconspicuously as possible, such that they seemed just more of the same but kicked up a notch – I watched from the sidelines and could scarcely believe my eyes. Nor did having my sight intact help me see how what were, to all appearances, steps taken in the dark could end up where they did, somewhere so fantastically precise – unless, that is, they were steps on a well-worn path down the abyss of history.

The people, meanwhile, before being wolfed by the state, had no choice but to swallow such propaganda whole, half-knowing that the idea behind it was not their happiness and well-being, but, rather, their heartless exploitation.

'At least they don't all gobble it up. It still has to be forced down their throats,' Chevauchet jeered half-heartedly, as though feeling sorry for his targets. 'Some still manage to quack out orations on the dignity of man. You know things are bad when the last shred of hope is a quacking duck! Quack of a duck! Quack-quack!'

Those who got on board voluntarily, CI helped look the other way. But the worst by far – the deadest ducks of all – were the token 'agitators' who blamed sloth and sleep for getting us into a Catch-22. Chevauchet foresaw a special place in hell for these 'useful idiots.' They were no better, and did more damage, than state apologists. 'We weren't vigilant enough,' they cried. 'We failed to sound the alarm to stop the seizure of power. But now we've been swung to the other extreme. This imposed wakefulness is our well-earned punishment. We didn't act when we still could. Narcoleptic children of Palinurus, we fell asleep at the helm, thinking instead of acting. And we lost control of the ship. We were not conscious enough to steer it. We were not awake enough to think. And now we are too awake to dream,' they scribbled, meekly sipping their daily dose of Potium.

Chapter Thirty-Four

One morning, I sat down in my habitual spot, feeling distinctly spectral and light-headed. I did not feel my body, but seemed to myself rather like the upright shades inhabiting the Fortunate Isles in Lucian's *True History.* Neither could I, going over in my mind our travels of the past year, tell those that were real from those that were imaginary. After all those waking hours spent with Chevauchet, I could not say for certain where dreams took over from reality and when they receded, or even which of the dreams were 'mine.' On this score, my memory failed me. But distinguishing between the real world and the dream world all of a sudden became important – clear in principle, if not in practice, to one not in the habit of self-policing.

In retrospect, I could see that my concern to know at least what was actual, genuine, or material arose from changes I had observed in Chevauchet. There were striking incongruities in his appearance and bearing. It began with glitches. In an instant, his face could morph from white to crimson, round to long, or his hair, ordinarily grey and straight as a die, curl and darken, as if animated. He would sometimes fade into the background, becoming transparent. Every so often, he turned on a dime without warning and reversed direction. And once, to my stupefaction, he advanced rectilinearly in cartwheels, displaying a level of agility one would never suspect in a man well into his seventies.

I put these momentary distortions of his image down to Prohibition. Although I concealed it from him, I worried lest he degrade further, or break down completely, and disappear from one day to the next.

We did have at least one serious conversation about the way things were going. It was he who brought it up. He was aware that his days were numbered. And time was running out for Onirica, unless he found a successor. Even at such moments, his wry sense of humour did not leave him:

'Only *homo somnians* could dream up *homo laborans,* this "new man" of theirs! If I am untimely, it's because the times are unmanly! All I can say is: lucky me!'

More troubling than his apparent incoherencies were the snags in his speech, which would become garbled or slurred; he might as well have been speaking a foreign language, for I could not make out anything. All I had then to orient me or get me out and back to the safety of my own consciousness were his gestures, as slow as a sloth's or as quick as a stealing monkey's, and the modulations of his voice (he maintained presence of mind throughout). At other times, lacunae formed, down which his words tumbled never to be reclaimed, or his speech simply suspended, as if words were failing him, and then, just as abruptly, fell over themselves to get out, sped up to the point of unintelligibility. When I first mentioned these events to him, he was nonplussed. Later, resigned, he would shrug and say 'they couldn't be helped.'

What of my own state? Peering back at me in the mirror were two dark-ringed globes, bleary and glassy like stagnant wells or ponds. I looked ill and underslept. But when I moved closer, I saw I had sleep in my eyes. And I felt fine – well, maybe somewhat depressed. Was the face in the mirror, then, my real face, or was it me through the haze of a dream – as in a looking-glass that was perpetually foggy? Was my breath still strong enough to fog a mirror? I wondered and brought my lips up to it. I breathed and blew on the glass until it began to turn opaque, clouding over. And as the mist dissipated, I saw something flash within it, like the scales of a fish that has come near the surface, or the gleam, in a dream, of a fulfilled wish.

Chapter Thirty-Five

Approximately two years after I met Chevauchet, we put our heads together to retaliate against Prohibition. The result was 'Operation Dormitory.' We had found a country house, close by yet isolated, large enough to sleep several dozen souls, and attainable entirely via an underground tunnel from the centre of the city (during the Great Public Works, the entrance was overlooked and never sealed off like the rest). Sleep was about to become illegal. What better moment to start organizing a resistance? In our minds we saw a reprise of the Maquis.

The practicalities took some figuring out. I had no qualms about benefitting personally from our endeavour. To charge for sleep was also the only way to signal its value. It would, moreover, allow me to be my own boss and work for a lost cause I believed in – possibly the last such cause. Since the circulation of money was tightly monitored, there was no question of taking any. The currency I honoured was local and outlawed. But it was payment in kind into a shared, mutual account. For the goods I received enabled me, and hence all who came to me, to survive.

Those who bought what I offered – rest – were desperate, husks of different shades, kept going by a cocktail sure to drive them mad, if it did not kill them first. They made enough to be able to 'afford' sleep from time to time, which is to say, they worked harder and all the more efficiently, in part thanks to furtively microdosing on sleep, in part because the idea of sleeping more by being able to buy more sleep pushed them to keep going at double speed, until, exhausted, they dragged themselves to me, untrackable below ground, vanishing like stones in water in central Paris, having taken every precaution and confident that they were not being tailed.

For them, I was the superfluous man, the invisible man, the disillusioned dreamer who had literally gone under.

As far as I know, I was the only 'Merchant of Sleep,' a sobriquet that stuck with me. What I sold was intangible and contraband. Though secret, it was not secrets. Though new, it was not information or news – nothing of the kind. I lent my clients the 'means of production' necessary to make what they needed to live. This means was a decent bed. What they 'produced' there was not a commodity. That made me a rentier, a hotelier. You could also say that I ran a workshop. But the goods leaving it were not the result of 'work' (contrary to what some would have). And, though ephemeral, they were inalienable from their 'producers.' These had it within themselves to make, in the safe space I provided, out of materials I did not provide, whatever their hearts desired and had time to spin.

Chapter Thirty-Six

In the factories, the desire to visit my Narcopolis formed like an escape plan inside a prison: meticulously, undeviatingly. The invitation and directions to the tunnel were passed down in Chinese whispers. But since this was not a game in which the exact message is eventually divulged, most who received it erred and never found their way, and the few who did I knew I could trust: they were serious, prudent, and attentive. Like a psychopomp, I led them into the underworld, and they followed me willingly to the ends of sleep.

Our meeting point was a cemetery, the Bastard family tomb. Its wrought-iron fence with finials of poppyheads was left open, the grille having been cut, and the mossy steps down through the burial vault were concealed by a slab that could be moved easily. If accidentally discovered, the mine shaft would attract only daredevils, served right by the treacherous deep. In the collective consciousness, the underground was life's sable lining, the literalization of hell, the concretion of eternal sleep. Old atlases of the subterranean network showed its reticular venation extending hundreds of kilometres. The charts had last been updated decades ago by amateur cataphiles; they were notorious for their errors and imaginary excavations, non-existent corridors that entrapped and confounded the casual, unseasoned explorer. To add to the fear they elicited, every few years a sinkhole would open suddenly beneath a house or a crowd standing in the street and, in an instant, like the yawn of a sleeping giant, inhale it entire. No sooner had the bodies been recovered than the mouth was filled again and paved over.

The secret passage to the château led through this web of galleries, threatening collapse at every step. It meandered beyond the outskirts of town into open country (though you would never know it down below). And, without my navigation, it was impassable. As there was no signage or markers to go by, I always had with me a compass, an extra miner's lamp, candles, and some matches. In certain sections, especially those of former limestone quarries, the ceilings were oppressively low. Frigidity and dankness, walls weeping and sooty from the days of torches, rhymed with the sepulchral dimensions to trigger claustrophobia, for which I also carried a remedy.

At about the four-hour mark, just when fatigue and panic began to overtake my followers, we would arrive at the destination. In imitation of the underground ossuary at the other end, I had ornamented the entrance lintel with a welcome message. *The Reason of Sleep Dispels Monsters.* Chiselled in the soft stone, the words waited for us, looking as though they had been there for centuries.

Shuffling after me, single file, up a narrow staircase, the newcomers trickled into the château's *cave,* or wine cellar. Anyone who stooped and felt diminished as they progressed now regained their full height, discovering that the hole through which they had entered was human-sized. In this musty vaulted hall – with two stacked chests for a desk (to which a repurposed wine cask made a not-unhandsome stool) – I had set up my office.

It was there that the registration and handover of the first installment, for so I had arranged the order of business, would take place. All would be recorded, including the names of each boarder and their exact donation. Since the food supply was not monitored, I accepted non-perishables in any quantity, and meat, fruit, and vegetables in limited amounts. Once everyone had been processed, I would explain the code. Not an ounce of Potium, smuggled in case one could not get to sleep, was allowed on the premises (to my credit, I did not do searches). I had, I reassured them, a homemade solution: the Sandman, an anti-Potium. It did the trick. Satisfaction guaranteed. I joked that anyone who didn't sleep like a baby was a monster.

With these formalities behind us, I conducted my strangers above ground, into the kitchen, where dormice mustered their winter hoard, and through the enfilade into the salon. It was just as Chevauchet and I had found it. Its dilapidation untouched, it seemed a sort of gathering place for shades, ghosts of the departed in a body but arrived from different eras. Open on the pianoforte was the sheet music for an orchestral work by Saint-Saëns. The instrument, the room's centrepiece, dominated the other furniture, which crowded around it: several armchairs, a gilded Louis XVI sofa, an Empire chaise longue with floral motifs, and a Directory escritoire, all dimly duplicated by a wall of corroded mirrors. Enhancing this chimerical arrangement, reminiscent of an upscale *brocante*, and heightening even more the attendant sense that invariably overcame me of having stepped into the past, was the lamentable condition of the objects themselves – especially the upholstery, the velvet no less than the silk and the toile, the drapes, curtains, and wall fabric – which time, in its relentless pursuit of entropy, had sun-faded, moth-riddled, and torn with the claws of resident mousers into long strips. The floor creaked prohibitively, and in many places the unwaxed parquet had either lifted or caved in. That, in its advanced decadence, it all held together was beyond me.

I remembered finding the atmosphere of quiet suspension unusually soporific. Life outside was largely denuded of old objects, which the authorities had judged a major public distraction, hence a potential cause of unrest. The past was a liability. Keeping it around was a hazardous proposition. Nothing to see in history's dry leaves! Keep going! Move along! *Circulez*!

From there, I led them upstairs to the sleeping gallery, furnished, in homage to opium dens, *à la chinoise*. (Their exhaustion was all the 'opium' needed by my guests.) Forty-one beds with clean grey sheets, blinds drawn tightly over the windows, and exposed Edison bulbs, for ambient lighting and their calming effect. Needless to say, none of this would have been possible without Chevauchet. Off Potium, up since five, and after long hours of feeling about underground, there and back, I had gone too long without rest.

'Go get some sleep,' Chevauchet would say to me when everyone else had retired. 'I can watch over them.' The forty-first bed was reserved for me.

Chapter Thirty-Seven

I awoke to find him gone. A regular sleeper, I was always the first to rise. Under my pillow, I discovered a leaf in Chevauchet's hand, like a direct transcription of my own mind:

A blank page still gives the right to dream, and language is the most potent illusionist.

Night never falls, its approach interminable. The cold sun sets the temper of our brutal times. Only in nature's course, or what is left of the seasons, does something like autumn shading into something like winter still have the right to its brushes and paints. We who still remark them want nothing more than to spin our waking thoughts into the phantasms of sleep, which extends our reflections by twisting and confusing them, making escape cables out of cobwebs and mazelike wildernesses out of orderly groves that keep us in check.

From the true black of night sprang both sleep and death. We may be sleeping on a bed of roses, yet their scent does not arouse their shape in our dreams. But this dullness of our senses is also a buffer, a defence. That which would be regrettable had we lain down in Paradise and could not feel it must be appreciated when we die to the world and must wake up in it. Once asleep, we are no longer alive to its ugliness, and its true horrors cannot touch us.

To keep my eyes open any longer is to act like our Antipodes, who on the other end of the transterrestrial tunnel strut upside down, and for whom we hang suspended like bats. Though the working classes were promised the world, and heaven with it, if they attained full consciousness of their material condition (whatever that meant), I find no such redemptive effect in nervous vigilance. The living the world over never sleep, yet their promised awakening is further off than ever. But at the hour that frees us from everlasting wakefulness, who will be alert? Who busy and restive on the night when sleep can at last hold sway and, as some have surmised, none shall ever wake again?

It was a farewell note, delivering on his notice that he would be leaving me.

We had had a bad fall. Chevauchet had hurt himself in the Pas de Loup, the Wolf Pass, among the more onerous climbs in these hypogean alps. After the accident, he had aged rapidly, doubling over like an old man without a cane. As his face grew waxen and haggard, and his gait moribund, I saw him, in the cold November drizzle, a scarecrow after a meagre harvest. Lost thus in a brown study, I read in his eyes that there would soon be nobody there.

At around the thirteenth hour, the first sleepers began to stir, and before long their chatting awakened the last, who took their time coming to, reluctant to let go of their dream sensations, wispy and evanescent like gossamer. I had, meanwhile, gone downstairs to lay the table, and presently announced that supper was waiting in the dining hall. The meal we owed to the previous parties, just as fare brought by the group about to sit down would feed the next. Kitchen duty I normally shared with Chevauchet, who made a mean chateaubriand. Proof we never begrudged them anything!

We ate by candlelight. I overheard one woman say she felt like a newborn, and that this must be the First Supper, heralding the Second Coming. Somebody else proclaimed sleep as the true Sabbath that will precipitate the Messianic Age – a remark I found more contrived than inspired. Listening to them go on, in broken silence, my thoughts darkened and took a morbid turn: 'This is all very well,' I said to myself, 'but if what you say is true, shouldn't one of you play the part of Judas?'

The moment had come for the balance to be rendered me for my services. I took out my pen and opened a large guest book, on whose cover I had tooled a cartouche of two swans with entwined necks. Then, one after another, I took down their dreams (or what remained of them), in the greatest possible detail, for safekeeping and posterity. These steadily accumulating volumes, I always prefaced, were a living archive, the future's *hypno-paideia*. In the fly-leaf of each book, I had copied out the same text, from Chevauchet:

> *Passerby, behold this monument in words as evidence that once upon a time there were dreams, and people who dreamt. If you take from this that people might dream again and begin to imagine it, then consider it done. For in you there is a dreamer.*

With this, our bargain was concluded: my dreamers got their sleep, and I their dreams.

The last dream recorded, it was time to head back if I were to make the meeting point by midnight to pick up a new group of visitors. Those I had fed, meanwhile, were about to put their life in my hands a second time. Without me (whom for this reason they also called 'the Old Mole'), and lacking suitable equipment, they would have groped their way, on the return journey, to certain death; so twisted and pitch-black were the tunnels, the murk in them so solid, they were as good as a blindfold. And if, despite the arduous trek, the tangible gloom sat well with my guests, so soothing and prolonging the sensation of sleep that they were grateful for it, it would plant on their lips a moist kiss, as, without a sunbeam to cut it, flooding every one of their arteries like embalming liquid, it made room for nothingness. There were no canaries in these mines to give them fair warning. Only faeries and dead ends.

A dead end of sorts from the outside, shuttered and padlocked, the château must have seemed uninhabited. For their sake, I never let my patrons venture outdoors to see the exterior. To the curious among them, I would say: 'And what if – just as with the Lutetian arena – the inside were all that was left?'

Chapter Thirty-Eight

Only a few still dared to close their eyes. In sleep that was fitful and irregular, dreams were not easy to come by; the arachnean work requisite for their meshing was impaired by a dreamer's distress, the fear of being discovered and rudely awakened. Without Chevauchet, I had the right, but no means of entry, to check on them. And that was just as well. For if these dreams were as frail as I suspected, I would worry about disturbing and damaging them.

It was much the same with daydreams. The disquiet of stolen sleep did not favour the relaxed semisomnous state, where reveries of revolt could be airborne without fear of being found out.

Among the men and women I helped, I noticed one particularly zealous, who came frequently. He always kept his distance, from what I guessed to be disdain or disgust; short, no longer young, invariably dressed in the same taupe wool suit, no matter the season, with hair the colour of charcoal, as dense and curly as a poodle's and suspended in a thunderhead over his face, which wore a sombre, splenetic expression, a darkling brew of suspicion, connivance, and spite; upon whose surface, simmering with chagrin or resentment, bubbled an evil eye. The more he failed to hide his bad temper and hostility from me (into whose good books he had every reason to want to ingratiate himself), giving by this to understand that he was motivated by misgivings as to my person – mutely accusing me, perhaps, of some dishonesty, or decoy, or of exposing him to poor hygiene in bug-infested beds – the more I responded in kind, with unconcealed antipathy and sidelong looks, judging his manner either a pose or a dodge, and trying him on false pretenses. He stood out as a studied outlier and had the makings less of a rebel than of a fanatic – if equally without a cause. His particulars only strengthened my impression of him. After some inquiries, I established that he went by the name of Max, claimed to be descended from his namesake – Robespierre – and, representing himself thus as a revolutionary by blood, had, for purely symbolic reasons, resided near the Place de la Bastille. Sleeping him brought me no satisfaction, not moral, not financial. My unease told me I was running a risk.

I may have been the only witness to the failure of Chevauchet's mission, which, with the end of sleep (de jure if not de facto) – and thus of dreaming, that sweet oblivion weighing down eyelids with beads of lead – had lost its raison d'être. As for the man himself, he vanished suddenly and without trace, just like that stone he had thrown the day of our meeting. As I stalked Paris's windswept, penumbral streets, the storefronts, in the throes of retail apocalypse, seemed to transmit his last message – which could also, it occurred to me, have been a message from reality to him. *Tout doit disparaître,* all must disappear, everything must go. Was it a sign of things to come? His unexplained absence confirmed that our time dreaming was up, that there was nothing to be done; the world had no further need of us, or dreams, or sleep. I should know: I was sleep's merchant. What I sold had value – was real, *existed* – as long as it was still worth the risk.

Tout doit disparaître. The familiar commercial slogan struck me particularly in its French wording. When no one comes into a store anymore, the goods inside become worthless, unreal. Whereupon they expire, which is to say, perish.

The apple does not fall far from the tree, and a rotten one even less! In Chevauchet's absence, refusing to come to terms with its finality and the futility of our mission, I redoubled my efforts and installed even more beds I had no problem filling nightly. And the regulars kept coming. They kept me busy. I made my bed, but not the time for it. Sleep beckoned, yet I ignored it. I would not accept that my human garden was full of rusty leaves and stones, from which nothing would sprout. How could I quit? Nighttime was for revolution.

Of course, expanding my operation only made it vulnerable to discovery. Sooner or later, I knew, I would be known to the authorities, and needed Chevauchet's advice, if only one last time.

Chapter Thirty-Nine

Inside the lining of my coat, where it slipped through a hole in the pocket, I found the calling card he had given me the day we met. I dialled the number written on it, hoping against hope that someone would pick up, and when no one did, headed for 11, Villa d'Enfer, the address of the embassy. I walked through the puddling rain as fast as my legs would carry me, and did not stop until, quite out of breath, I rang the unmarked doorbell on a discreet and undistinguished facade. I had a memory of a door in my mind – an ethereal image that I didn't trust myself ever having seen in reality, and of which the door in front of me was not the very picture.

I heard the floor behind it creak, and a middle-aged woman opened. By her mournful, wilted mien, I reckoned she must have been a nurse, a domestic, or a personal secretary, retained by an attachment in the empty space wherein she greeted me. It was almost as if she were planted – a cipher – for those foolish enough to think they could get to the bottom of things. And without asking so much as my name or what business I had coming there and looking so bedraggled, she let me in.

Peaceful, bathed in light filtered through stained glass set in four vertical windows, the sitting room to which I was shown would have made a charming chapel. The modest collection of art, furniture, and other objects assembled inside complicated this first impression with its apparent randomness. A sculpture of Atlas with a pretty patina had been placed upon a pedestal beneath a neoclassically framed reproduction of *The Depths of the Sea,* a watercolour by Edward Burne-Jones. Above the writing table hung a Daumier print, eyed from across the room by a Senufo mask, most certainly a modern copy. A squat and smart sofa, whose unembarrassed redness was a kind of *profiteor,* sat offset by white wainscoting, against which, closer to the door, a dark armoire – a piece of latter-day *chinoiserie* – rose awkwardly, as if to indicate an exit or entrance to another dimension.

Seeking something to occupy me, my eyes alighted on a book. It was *A Dream of John Ball.* The title sounded vaguely familiar; was not the author the utopian anarchist responsible for *News from Nowhere*? I leafed through it slowly and happened upon this marked passage, worthy of being put on a tombstone:

> *I pondered all these things, and how men fight and lose the battle, and the thing that they fought for comes about in spite of their defeat, and when it comes turns out not to be what they meant, and other men have to fight for what they meant under another name ...*

I held the volume in my hand, or rather: there it rested, the weight and solidity of an old edition. My attention then turned to the leather binding, and I admired its beauty and artistry. The cover depicted a large closed eyelid, executed in polychrome marquetry. It was clearly the work of a master craftsman, bringing to mind my late friends, of whom one was a gifted bookmaker. I recognized her genius in the design.

While I waited in vain for someone to fetch me, the sun setting through the windows sapped their blues, roses, and yellows and, little by little, submerged me in darkness. Finding no light switch, I got up for the small menorah I had seen upon the marble mantelpiece, between scaled-down replicas of the Rosetta Stone and the heads of two Cycladic idols.

It was then, the candles lit, that by the shadow it cast upon the bare wall I first took notice of the tall hourglass. Looming ominous atop the armoire, lonely and lopsided, its curves trembling in the candlelight, it had none of the dance of death's rigid boniness.

Chapter Forty

I opened the wardrobe and heard dogs barking somewhere down the tunnel, within earshot but still far off. Inclining inward, I felt a mortuary wind caress my face. My eyelid twitched uncontrollably. Some moments later, the closet shook violently as a three-strong posse of policemen clambered through the frame and spilled out like actors from the wings, the animals thrusting their muzzles between their legs, wild with excitement. I had left the door ajar, for I could not bear them breaking it down.

I was awake and ready. I held my arms high over my head as they searched me, then the room, for weapons. That done, they demanded to be taken to the sleeping quarters. Obedient, I nevertheless chose the 'scenic route' – through the horseshoe-shaped garden – that the sunset might enchant them, and they would go easy on my guests. The weather was mild, the leaves, only just nipped by the first frost, had yet to turn. The majestic crabapple tree, *Malus sylvestris,* had dropped its ripe fruit, there being no one to pick it, and from the soil around it there rose a sweet odour of decomposition.

We entered the long gallery, where the air was stale and heavy with respiration. The sleepers, dead to the commotion, dreamt on peacefully, or, fearing what might happen to them when they woke up, feigned sleep. From some the blanket had slid or been thrown off, revealing a contortion of limbs, no two bodies in the same position. In repose, they were angelic and beautiful.

Meanwhile, the gendarmes tore through the hall with a terrific din, the dogs sniffing, snarling, and baring their armature to show who was in charge.

'Wake them up!' ordered the officer closest to me.

I said I could not.

'Why's that?'

'Can't be done. They wake up when they wake up.'

'You're lying! Without you they'd sleep for days. They miss a dose of Potium and they're out like a light. They can't afford to stay here indefinitely. How much does a scoundrel like you make off them? Come on, what do they pay you?'

'That's between me and them. And I don't charge by the hour. I let them sleep however much they need or like. They're paying customers. And as long as they can afford it, I'm here to feed the addiction.'

'Filthy Jewrab!' the officer sneered at me.

'They are safe here,' I continued coolly, pretending not to have heard the compliment. 'No one looked for them – until now, that is. That you should come this far on your own, without an insider, is next to impossible. So, tell me, how did you get wind of me? Who brought you all this way?'

And as I confronted him, I thought I recognized the scowl – the sullen aspect and tenebrous complexion that went so consummately with it – *magni nominis umbra*, in the dogged shadow of a great name, his coveted Jacobin ancestry – I knew it well, that face in search of a death mask and a place in the annals of ignominy. He always slept, this one, with his lids parted just a crack, like those of the deceased; what I had mistaken for a sign of lagophthalmos was in fact watchfulness. My intuition about him had indeed hit the mark.

Max the blue, true-blue Max, did not appreciate my backtalk and ordered the other two to wake up the sleepers, if necessary by force. They flew like furies from bed to bed, shouting and kicking the footboards. The results of this obnoxious conduct were negligible. Some figures stirred and changed position. But my forty heroes kept sleeping, like ones enchanted, making music with their snoring, groaning, and sighing, as if in defiance of their would-be tormentors, who yelled:

'We'll fix them good, your sleeping dogs, so that they'll *never* wake up! You'd like that, wouldn't you?!'

Their bodies padded like cells, they criss-crossed the hall corner to corner, rifling through everything.

'Stop it, stop at once! You won't get anywhere this way.' I felt an acute responsibility to protect my patrons, as their guardian. I had with me the key to a box of ivory and horn, containing the Sandman, a powerful sedative. But its whiteness gave it away.

'Keep your rotten hands off that thing!' the officer barked. 'Now, or you're done for! And the world's one scum cleaner.'

And they fell to dragging the sleepers one by one out of their beds, beating them blindly at the least show of resistance. These were bad cops, rabid and savage.

'Look at 'em clowns!' It was the ringleader again. He was having fun, laughing his head off. 'That's what you get for not taking your medicine! Get moving, junkies!' and, addressing his confreres, 'Let's go!'

They rounded us up, still comatose some, and amused themselves pinching and prodding us with their guns in sensitive places. Then, Max taking the lead, they shoved and pushed us, a flock without a shepherd, handcuffed and linked in a chain gang, into and down the passageways leading back to the capital.

Their haste was their undoing. They soon realized they had no choice but to trust me, to let me guide them. Below, they could not force me to do anything. They had entered at their own risk, and I, pretending to obey them, went about gaining the upper hand. Instead of making good time, as they must have thought, we strayed deeper into tapering territory I knew to be well-nigh impenetrable, sans issue. We made one after another vertiginous descent. Dreamily, as one picking flowers, I took us where peril was writ large, to the edges of cunicular cliffs. I played at losing my way.

Through the entire ordeal, I was careful to a fault, awaiting an opportunity to give them the slip. They would have to fend for themselves. Some would go mad. All the better. I no longer cared, shedding all remorse. Indefatigable, I made a truce with the demon stirring inside me. I had to think of the future so as not to lose sleep over it. I had to get away. And, as in an autoscopic transcendent projection I saw myself neither unsung nor a hero, a change came over me.

Plenty mortified, the cops wanted to stop and regroup, to work out what course to take. They had had quite enough of this 'scandal.' Now, now or never. It was my only chance.

I took off, and as I fled, I heard the discharge of a firearm behind me, then a loud rumbling, the earth vibrating all around … And none too soon, as far as I was concerned.

There are tragedies, and there are tragedies. Some wait to strike till the intermission.

Chapter Forty-One

Over the entrance to the Palace of Justice, commanding its classical Greek frieze, stands Argus Panoptes, the guardian who never sleeps, every one of his hundred eyes open. Above it, there is a Latin inscription, which reads *MALUM DORMIT*, Evil sleeps. It is a perversion of an old proverb – the Devil *never* sleeps. Not so long ago, Evil never slept. It was Good that closed its eyes. But such an image of Good was not right for the times. Good should be sleepless and ever-watchful.

My mind is captive, my walk as free as can be. I have received the maximum penalty, a week without sleep. But judging by the ghastly state of the poor devil on the bench beside me, ciliatomized several days ago, each day more hallucinatory and convulsive than the last, a week will likely be the end of me. It is a death sentence in everything but name. This is what they do to enemies of the state and mass murderers. Prosecuted for seditious conspiracy, trafficking, and triggering the collapse of an old tunnel, killing many, I was convicted on all counts. My genealogical data was scoured for aberrant, criminal individuals. And, lo and behold, they found one: a homosexual, anarchist assassin of an American president! Unlike him, I had no Emma

Goldman to defend me. Not that it did him any good. Like me, the bastard called himself 'Nobody.' Thanks to the unfailing apparatus of justice, I was reconnected with him – my distant double, pages apart in the history books.

I serve my sentence in a portable prison. The agent for sleep deprivation, which makes life endurable, is denied convicts, evildoers like me. Only those who are technically at liberty have access to it. And where everyone is a watcher and every watcher is watched at all times, there can be no black market for drugs. Using them would lighten the punishment and relieve the prisoner. And relieved prisoners are virtually free. To give us Potium would amount to an amnesty.

The only time sleep is permitted is when one is already lying in state. For they don't call it death anymore, or necrosis, but *narcosis* – *terminal narcosis* – which seals the evil of sleep.

The forced wakefulness without reprieve is a strange reversal of death, because deadlier than it.

Chapter Forty-Two

Two days ago, I opened my eyes for the last time. After I had been detained, the guards, one of whom was familiar, let me sleep for weeks. A great clandestine gift: freedom in the bowels of a prison hospital. I felt freer in this bastille than at liberty. What heavenly bliss it was to be nursed by sleep. So I closed my eyes every night, knowing full well it could not be much longer. I would shut each of them tightly, as though sliding the lid over a manhole (a hole big enough for a man to dream in it) from beneath. And I would plumb more profoundly than ever into my dream.

The swans, I have been watching them closely. They are floating toward each other, necks extended, then twining together like rope. The black ones have multiplied, the white have all but disappeared. Perhaps they strangled themselves and drowned. Do swans still dream? They come so near now, and the still, reflective pool in which they float this way and that only distantly resembles water. It is pure reflection, unrippled, like a pale sky, a white wall, or a blank sheet of paper. When the sun comes out over the pond, the swans seem more like specks of dust on a light table, or particles viewed under a microscope. And as I move my eyes to get a clearer picture, they evade my gaze. Their gliding accompanies me everywhere.

'These are no swans,' I hear Chevauchet say.

What are they, then? But whenever my mind starts to drift, someone can be counted on to grab me by the shoulder with their 'Hey you!' 'Wake up, citizen!' 'No sleeping!' – by which they mean no dreaming, of any kind. They are just ordinary passersby, citizens doing their duty to the state.

I look up and see the birds floating now across the sky – or is it my eyes? And I put in a few drops of snow for relief.

'They're not birds; they're *mouches*,' whispers Chevauchet, 'flying flies.'

I look out at the lake, which has frozen over. In permanent winter, nothing floats, nothing grows, nothing shades (not one willow weeping). It is the same with the rest of the world when the centre has a lock on the sun. The world is an eyeball in space, which nothing protects.

Upon lidless eyes flies soon come to rest. But the corpse in whose orbits they will lay their eggs has seen happiness.

The most private and unknowing wishful thinking is to be preferred to unconscious walking in Indian file; because it can be informed.

– Ernst Bloch

Drunken with realism, the psychologists insist too heavily on the escape element of our reveries. They do not always recognize that reverie weaves soft bonds around the dreamer, that reverie is a 'binding,' and, in short, that in the strictest sense of the term, it 'poetizes' the dreamer.

– Gaston Bachelard

That violence is not the result of conditions only, but also largely depends upon man's inner nature, is best proven by the fact that while thousands loath tyranny, but one will strike down a tyrant. What is it that drives him to commit the act, while others pass quietly by? It is because the one is of such a sensitive nature that he will feel a wrong more keenly and with greater intensity than others.... The cause for such an act lies deeper, far too deep for the shallow multitude to comprehend. It lies in the fact that the world within the individual, and the world around him, are two antagonistic forces, and, therefore, must clash.

– Emma Goldman

About the Author

S. D. Chrostowska teaches in the Department of Humanities and in the Graduate Program in Social and Political Thought at York University in Toronto. She is the author of the collection of fragments *Matches: A Light Book* (punctum, 2015; second expanded ed., 2019), of the epistolary novel *Permission* (Dalkey Archive, 2013), and of a history of literary criticism, *Literature on Trial* (University of Toronto Press, 2012). She has also co-edited a volume of essays, *Political Uses of Utopia: New Marxist, Anarchist, and Radical Democratic Perspectives* (Columbia University Press, 2017). A French translation of *Matches*, with a foreword by the German filmmaker and writer Alexander Kluge, was published by Belles Lettres-Klincksieck in 2019. Prof. Chrostowska's essays and fiction have appeared in BOMB, *The Believer, The Review of Contemporary Fiction, The Hedgehog Review,* and elsewhere. She has contributed scholarly articles to such journals as *diacritics, New German Critique, Public Culture, New Literary History, SubStance,* and *boundary 2*. She is currently finishing a modern history of German and French critical social theory.

Typeset in Arno.

Printed at the Coach House on bpNichol Lane in Toronto, Ontario, on Zephyr Antique Laid paper, which was manufactured, acid-free, in Saint-Jérôme, Quebec, from second-growth forests. This book was printed with vegetable-based ink on a 1973 Heidelberg KORD offset litho press. Its pages were folded on a Baumfolder, gathered by hand, bound on a Sulby Auto-Minabinda and trimmed on a Polar single-knife cutter.

Edited by Tamara Faith Berger and Alana Wilcox
Designed by Crystal Sikma
Cover art 'Le jour est un grand ours' by Jean-Pierre Paraggio
Cover and interior design by Crystal Sikma

Coach House Books
80 bpNichol Lane
Toronto ON M5S 3J4
Canada

416 979 2217
800 367 6360

mail@chbooks.com
www.chbooks.com